Yukon River Ghost

Yukon River Ghost

A Girl's Ghost Town Adventure

MacBride Museum Yukon Kids Series

Keith Halliday

Illustrations by Pascale Halliday and Aline Halliday

iUniverse, Inc.

New York Bloomington Shanghai

Yukon River Ghost
A Girl's Ghost Town Adventure

Copyright © 2008 by Keith Halliday

iUniverse books may be ordered through booksellers or by contacting:

iUniverse
1663 Liberty Drive
Bloomington, IN 47403
www.iuniverse.com
1-800-Authors (1-800-288-4677)

Because of the dynamic nature of the Internet, any Web addresses or links contained in this book may have changed since publication and may no longer be valid.

This is a work of fiction. All of the characters, names, incidents, organizations, and dialogue in this novel are either the products of the author's imagination or are used fictitiously.

All images and photos are © 2008 by Keith Halliday, except for images generously provided by the MacBride Museum or as noted otherwise.

ISBN: 978-0-595-49364-7 (pbk)
ISBN: 978-0-595-61071-6 (ebk)

Printed in the United States of America

To my daughter Pascale
With thanks to Oscar Wilde

Contents

Foreword . . . . *ix*

Journal #1 1

Journal #2 7

Journal #3 14

Journal #4 21

Journal #5 28

Journal #6 35

Journal #7 42

Journal #8 48

Journal #9 53

Journal #10 58

Journal #11 62

Journal #12 67

Journal #13 72

Journal #14 77

Aurore's journal 83

Journal #15 87

Journal #16 91

Journal #17 98

About This Book *101*

Acknowledgments *103*

About the Author *105*
About the Illustrators *107*
About the MacBride Museum *109*
Also available in the MacBride Museum Yukon Kids Series *111*

Foreword

This 1902 journal was written by a remarkable young Yukon pioneer named Papillon Dutoit. In it, she describes her startling adventures at Canyon City on the banks of the Yukon River, while also giving us a unique look at the ups and downs of life for Yukon kids as the great Klondike gold rush petered out.

Papillon's story is the third in the series that historians now call the "Aurore papers."

The first to be discovered was the 1898 Chilkoot Trail diary of Aurore Dutoit, Papillon's step-sister. She was a young girl from Montreal who found herself swept up in an unexpected adventure with notorious Alaskan bandit Soapy Smith at the height of the Klondike gold rush.

The second was written by Papillon's brother Kip five years later. It chronicled previously unknown espionage and diplomatic intrigue on the Alaskan frontier during the 1903 Alaska-Canada border dispute, including the secret visit of President Theodore Roosevelt to Skagway.

This journal, published here as Yukon River Ghost, is of equal historical significance. It is a unique first-hand account of life in the Yukon after the Klondike gold rush ended and the Yukon once again seemed like an empty place.

Like the original Aurore diary, this journal was found in an old trunk in the family cabin near Marsh Lake. It was carefully wrapped in moose hide with a personal note from Papillon herself.

We don't know why Papillon hid her journal away instead of publishing it. She was well known later in the Yukon as a story teller, entertaining years of girl guide camps and story nights around the campfire. But she never told this one, even though her note says all the events actually happened. Perhaps the final scene provides a clue.

Our team of historians has done a minimum of editing. We have corrected some spellings, including modern spellings for place names. For example, Whitehorse instead of White Horse. All the photos and drawings found with the journal had a short note from Papillon on the back. We have included these as captions under each one. Otherwise, the journal is how Papillon left it when she wrapped it in moose hide and put it in that now famous trunk.

There is one final point that we must make as historians. We have checked all the facts. Everything Papillon describes at Canyon City is historically accurate. Characters such as Will Drury of Taylor & Drury merchants are verifiable and events such as Jack London's passage through Whitehorse actually happened. And a man did disappear in Miles Canyon on that fateful evening of July 11th, 1902.

But we cannot, of course, verify Papillon's repeated descriptions of a ghost on the Yukon River.

We will leave that to readers, especially any who have watched the mist roll into Miles Canyon on a crisp Yukon summer morning.

Professor H. I. Story
Whitehorse, Yukon Territory
2008

Journal #1

June 29th, 1902
Canyon City, Yukon Territory
**In my sleeping robe and so early in the morning only some of
the birds are awake**

Have you ever told people something you knew was true and they
didn't believe you?

It happens to me a lot.

"What an imagination you have, Papillon!" they say. Or "That's
nice, Papillon." My teacher Miss Conrad says "Thanks for sharing!"
when what she really means is "Stop bothering me and get back to
your boring handwriting practice."

It happened three times on the last day of school. First, I heard
one of the boys at recess telling his friends that Cheddar cheese
came from orange cows. When I told them it was really from a town
called Cheddar in England, he got really mad. He snarled at me like
an angry husky and chased me across the schoolyard and down
Lambert Street.

After that, I told Miss Conrad that I'd seen her best friend kissing
that handsome new police constable behind the bank the day
before. I don't know why, but she got all upset and told me to stop
making up stories. Then she made our whole class redo our hand-

writing while she sat at her desk staring out the window and dabbing tears with her handkerchief like she had a speck of dust in her eye or something.

And then, when I got home, everyone accused me of giving the steak we were going to eat for dinner to our dog D'Artagnan. They were so upset I grabbed my book, climbed the tree behind the house and read in my secret spot until bedtime.

Well, I guess that last one is a bit different since it really was me who gave the steak to D'Artagnan. A dog needs a steak every now and then. I don't think my family needed to get so upset about having just potatoes and mushy peas, even if it was our last dinner at home before hiking to Canyon City for the summer.

Anyway, you can imagine how they would react if I told them I saw a ghost this morning.

They would tell me it's impossible to see ghosts. Especially adults, who seem to specialize in telling you what you can't do.

And they would be wrong of course, because I did see a ghost this morning at Miles Canyon.

We were sleeping in Papa's favourite old canvas tent. There were Papa and Maman, my sister Aurore and my brothers Kip and Yves. Maman is really my step-mother since my mother died when I was little. Papa and Maman got married during the gold rush. I guess that's four years ago now.

It also means that Yves and Aurore are really my step-brother and step-sister.

Fortunately, I'm not a princess in Europe so I don't have to put up with any of that evil step-mother stuff. Maman is wonderful and I love having Aurore and Yves in the family.

Most of the time, anyway. You know how brothers and sisters are.

Our dog D'Artagnan was there too. He's named after the hero of the Three Musketeers. We all like playing musketeers. I like how they always helped each other and said "All for one and one for all!"

Aurore always pretends she's one of Queen Anne's secret agents. Yves and Kip mostly like the sword fighting parts.

Our two workhorses Cardinal and Milady were there too. Outside, not in the tent of course.

We spend every summer in the bush, helping Papa cut wood for the winter. He says it's how he "makes a living," which means it's how he pays for our family's food, clothes and everything else we need. He cuts firewood for lots of people in Whitehorse, including the big Taylor & Drury store and the church.

It's hard work, but everybody needs firewood in the winter so he's always busy. We have to help because people don't pay as much for firewood as they used to during the gold rush. And our family needs every extra bit of money we can earn.

Papa had picked Canyon City for this summer. It has lots of wood. It's right beside Miles Canyon, which means it's just up the Yukon River from Whitehorse. It's easy to get the wood back to town on the old gold rush tramway trail. That's why we had Cardinal and Milady with us.

Nobody lives at Canyon City now. But four years ago during the Klondike gold rush it was full of people![1]

Anyway, I woke up shivering just as it was starting to get light. It was cold even though it was summer. Maman and Papa were fast asleep under Papa's buffalo robe. Yves and Aurore were snuggled warmly on either side of D'Artagnan. Kip was all turned around with his feet on D'Artagnan too.

---

1.   Editor's Note: Canyon City was a gold rush boom town. So many people set out for the Klondike gold fields that they were known as "stampeders." In 1898 tens of thousands of them took the Chilkoot Pass or White Pass and then floated to Dawson City on the Yukon River. At Canyon City they would stop and portage their goods around Miles Canyon, the Devil's Punchbowl and the White Horse Rapids. It was about 10 kilometres from Canyon City to Whitehorse where the river became safe again. Two tramways were built along the route. In 1900, the White Pass railway reached Whitehorse and Canyon City quickly became a ghost town.

"It's a two dog night," I said to myself, wishing we had another dog to keep me warm.

I sat up and looked around. It was very early in the morning and the dawn light was a strange colour coming in between the flaps of the tent. I could hear everyone breathing quietly.

Sometimes brothers and sisters are most loveable when they are asleep.

I smiled at them for a second, then quietly got up and slipped outside. It was beautiful and quiet. The river poured quickly past Canyon City with hardly a sound. A little family of ducks came into sight, floated past and disappeared in the blink of an eye.

I watched the Yukon River go by and wondered why it is always in such a hurry.

Somehow it came into my head that I should walk along the river. Eventually I stopped and sat down on the side of Miles Canyon. It was right at that big rock, beside the spot where the river suddenly gets narrow and funnels into the stony walls of the canyon.

It was cold in the morning even though it was summer. I shivered and wished I had brought my coat. The air was perfectly clear. I could see Grey Mountain behind me as clearly as through a telescope. On the river, there were just a few wisps of fog close to the water.

I was looking upstream, wondering what it was like when Papa first came down the river during the gold rush. He told me that more than two hundred boats were wrecked in the rapids. That's why Papa never made it to the gold in Dawson City. He knew all about rivers and guided hundreds of people through the rapids after Sam Steele and the North West Mounted Police made it a law that you couldn't go through without a guide.

Suddenly, I noticed the fog. There was more of it than just a second before. As it got close to the mouth of the canyon, it started to come together.

To my amazement, the fog pulled together into a shape.

It was like a canoe with a man in it!

I blinked. The fog-man was paddling. Not frantically like a cheechako[2]. But carefully, like he'd known how to paddle canoes forever. The fog-canoe started to twist sideways in the current, but a few quick paddle strokes and it was straight again.

The fog-man looked up. He looked surprised to see me. In fact, I thought he looked a little guilty as if I'd caught him doing something he wasn't supposed to. He looked very serious for a second. He took a hand off his paddle and tipped his hat to me. It was very polite, just like Sam Steele used to do it. Then he started paddling furiously as the canoe headed into the rapids.

I watched in amazement. The water roared against the stony canyon walls. Just when you thought the canoe would smash into a rock or disappear under a giant wave, the fog-man would make a few quick paddle strokes and the canoe would sweep into safer water. Just as the canoe went out of sight, I saw the ghost—somehow I knew by then that it was a ghost—take his hand off the paddle again. He waved his hat in the air and shouted "yippee" as he disappeared into the roaring spray of the Devil's Punchbowl at the bottom of the canyon.

I looked around. The first ray of sunlight flashed onto the top of Grey Mountain. The fog was suddenly gone from the river.

I heard a soft noise and suddenly noticed a raven. He was a big old one. He was standing on the side of the canyon not ten feet from me. Even more strangely, he was completely white!

I stared at him.

He stared back. Then he tilted his head to one side. It was if he was saying, "What? Haven't you seen a ghost before?"

Then he flew across the river and disappeared.

---

2.   Editor's note: A "cheechako" is an aboriginal word for a tenderfoot or inexperienced newcomer. It remains widely used in the Yukon, as are other First Nations words such as "potlatch" and "skookum." Experienced old timers are known as Sourdoughs.

Above: Miles Canyon, where I first saw the ghost.
You can see a boat headed for the Devil's Punchbowl in the background.

Photo courtesy of MacBride Museum (1989-3-341).

Journal #2

June 29th, 1902
Canyon City, Yukon Territory
Hiding behind the old police cabin just before lunch

After I saw the ghost, I ran back to our tent and slipped quietly under the covers. I was too excited to sleep at first, so I lay under the blanket and wrote in my journal. But the next thing I knew I could hear the crackle of the campfire. Between the flaps of the tent I could see my big brother Kip blowing softly on the fire to get the kindling started. In the background, I could hear my little brother Yves complaining that he always had to get the wood in the morning.

Then I saw my sister Aurore's boots and saw her put down two buckets of water. The flap of the tent flew open. "Get up, sleepyhead!" she said. "Stop lollygagging. Everyone is done their chores except you, and it's *your* turn to get out the plates and forks." She's two years older than me and thinks she's the boss.

"I don't remember *you* doing the dishes last night," I pointed out as I quickly closed my journal and stuffed it into my bag.

Maman cleared her throat and held out a stack of plates for me. "Les assiettes, ma chouette," she said. "Assiettes" means "plates" and "ma chouette" means "my little sweetie." We speak French with Maman because her English isn't very good. Papa's is much better. But Maman can still tell when we are bickering no matter what language it's in.

I could see Yves running around. He was supposedly collecting kindling for the fire, but suddenly he shouted "en garde" like a musketeer and attacked Kip with one of his sticks! Kip fought back with a broom handle until they were both rolling in the dirt.

Maman sighed and flipped the pancakes.

I opened the kitchen box and handed out the plates, knives, forks and cups. Then I took my place beside the fire. Maman took a sourdough pancake from the big pan and put it on my plate. Suddenly, the boys were sitting quietly beside me holding their plates politely.

Maman gave each of them a huge pancake too. And for a treat, we even got a slice of bacon!

It was really good. A camprobber flew into the tree right beside me and watched carefully, hoping I would drop something.

That reminded me about the white raven and the ghost. I couldn't wait to tell everyone. I opened my mouth to speak but Papa tapped me on the shoulder and pointed at the jam. "Papillon, la confiture, s'il te plaît," he said. I watched him spread it all over his pancakes. I knew he was about to tell us about how back in New Brunswick his uncle made maple syrup every spring and they had as much as they wanted for their pancakes.

I love those stories. "I would love to try maple syrup someday," I said.

"There aren't any maple trees in the Yukon," replied Aurore in her bossy voice. "And besides, it's very expensive."

"Maybe we could make syrup out of pine trees. We have lots of those."

Papa laughed. "Papillon, if you make syrup out of pine sap you get turpentine and that's poisonous!" he said. I don't think he meant it in a mean way. But I felt my face go red anyway. Why did I always say the wrong thing? I looked down at my pancakes. I decided to tell them about the ghost later.

Kip stuffed a whole pancake into his mouth. "Gurble pik ice cabn?" he sputtered, before gulping down his cup of water and looking around for more pancakes.

"Ça n'était ni le français ni l'anglais," observed Maman pointedly, saying that he was speaking neither English nor French when his mouth was full.

Kip swallowed his whole pancake in an enormous gulp. I thought I could hear it fall down his throat and splash into his stomach a foot below.

"Excuse-moi," he said to Maman. "Can I pick the cabin we're going to stay in?"

"We'll pick it together," laughed Papa with a smile.

"Are we really allowed to pick any cabin?" asked Yves. "Don't other people own them?"

"Yves," said Aurore. "This is a ghost town. That means all the cabins are abandoned. Nobody owns them. We'll just pick the nicest and clean it up for ourselves for the summer."

"The Law of the Yukon says we should just leave it in better shape than we found it," said Papa. "You know," he continued, pouring some canned milk into his coffee, "all these cabins used to be bustling with people. Canyon City used to be way bigger than Whitehorse. Everybody had to stop here and portage their gear around Miles Canyon, the Devil's Punchbowl and the White Horse rapids."

"Why not run right through?" asked Kip. He'd heard the story a hundred times, but he liked to encourage Papa.

Papa laughed. "You wouldn't want to lug all your gear 35 miles over the Chilkoot Pass just to lose it when your raft flipped in the river! Once all the gear was on shore, I used to guide the boats through the rapids. They say 50,000 people went through here, and I guided lots of 'em. The famous author, Jack London, for example!"[1]

"Why don't they come through any more?"

"They built the railway to Whitehorse. No one wants to risk their lives in Miles Canyon anymore. Plus the gold rush is over. All the stampeders went off to Nome, Alaska when they found gold there."

All the people were gone now, I thought. Except us. It seemed a bit sad when you saw the old boats up on the shore or a cabin with a roof falling in.

On the other hand, as Papa said, we didn't have to share the Yukon River with so many yahoos any more!

So, after breakfast, we left our tent and walked through the old cabins at Canyon City to choose one to live in for the summer. It had only been a few years, but already some were falling down. Papa said it was because they built them in such a hurry during the gold rush.

I found one that looked great. A sign read "Hotel" in big painted letters on the front. "Hey everyone!" I shouted. "I've always wanted to live in a hotel." The others ran over and I pushed open the door.

Everyone laughed. "Nice hotel!" said Aurore sarcastically. "It doesn't have a roof!"

"Or even walls!" added Kip.

They were right. Behind the door was just more dirt with some young willows growing in it.

"I remember this place!" laughed Papa. "It was just a big tent. They built a wooden front to make it look nice but they never got around to the walls."

We soon found the best cabin. It said "Lucky Eight Mine" on the front. It had three rooms, its roof was in good shape and it even had wooden floors and glass in its windows.

---

1.   Editor's Note: The famous author Jack London did pass through Canyon City and Whitehorse on his way to the Klondike. Whitehorse pioneer Antoine Cyr is also reported to have piloted him through the rapids. Aurore and Yves also met him and, as described in *Aurore of the Yukon*, it appears their dog D'Artagnan was London's model for Buck in *Call of the Wild*.

"Hard Luck Henry says don't stay there!" said a raspy but friendly voice behind us. It was an old Sourdough prospector, leaning on his walking stick. He had a bushy grey beard and a grin that showed a few gaps where some bush dentist had done his work. His clothes were torn, his hat was faded, and his pack seemed to hold everything he owned. He didn't look unhappy though. He coughed, spit and smiled at us. "That cabin's haunted. Hard Luck Henry knows."

"Who's Hard Luck Henry?" asked Yves.

"You're lookin' right at 'im, boy!"

Yves looked puzzled. Aurore whispered. "*He* is Hard Luck Henry. He never says 'I' because it's bad luck." Yves still looked puzzled. "A lot of time in the bush. Alone. With no one to talk to," she added, twirling her finger in the air beside her head when Hard Luck Henry wasn't looking.

Papa walked around the corner. "Oh hello Henry! Any colours in your pan this time?" That's slang talk for "Did you get any gold?" They shook hands.

"No, sirree. Hard Luck Henry's still got his nickname. So far, anyways." He winked at me when he said "so far." I could tell he was hinting that he might have found a good creek. But if he had, he wasn't telling us. He coughed again. "Was just on the trail for town and saw your kids. Was tellin' 'em not to stay in this cabin. Haunted."

"Haunted!" exclaimed Papa.

"Yes, sirree. Belonged to Alastair Riveridge and that—" He looked at us. "That fellow Rufus Slight. When they were mining across the river a few years back. Slight moved out after Alastair disappeared in the Devil's Punchbowl. Been haunted ever since. A few fellas been back to look for Alastair's gold cache, but no one's found it."

"Wow! A ghost!" exclaimed Yves.

Papa smiled. "Aren't all the ghosts busy in Europe in all those castles and dungeons?"

Hard Luck Henry smiled back. "Where there's people, there's wicked people. And where there's wicked people, there's ghosts.

Especially when there's gold caches that ain't been found. And especially, especially when those gold caches got a famous nugget shaped like a lucky eight." He laughed. "And anyways, you can't have a ghost town without a ghost. And Canyon City sure is a ghost town." That seemed to prove it as far as Hard Luck Henry was concerned.

Suddenly he turned and looked at me. I don't know why. "Now missee, you know as well as Hard Luck Henry that the ghost didn't move to Whitehorse with the rest of the folks when Canyon City closed up. Why don't you tell your Papa and brothers and sisters?"

I didn't know what to say. Because they never believed me? I looked down at my feet.

Papa put his arm around my shoulder. "Well," he said, "the ghosts'll just have to share it with us this summer. You know how it is with us Sourdoughs! Too much wood to cut, gravel to pan and bacon to fry to worry about ghosts!"

"Well, it's your Hallowe'en I guess. Don't say Hard Luck Henry didn't warn you."

Above: Canyon City, Yukon Territory before it became a ghost town!
You can see the wooden tramway to Whitehorse.
Our cabin is in the background.

Photo courtesy of MacBride Museum (1989-4-813)

Journal #3

June 30th, 1902
Canyon City, Yukon Territory
Writing in our new cabin at breakfast time on a table made of butter boxes

After Hard Luck Henry got back on the trail to Whitehorse, we pulled open the door to the cabin and had a look.

I was the last one to step in. I looked around. It looked surprisingly tidy for an abandoned cabin. But it felt a bit strange. "Like a ghost?" I said to myself. But I didn't know what a ghost felt like. The others seemed already to have forgotten about Hard Luck Henry.

"The squirrels haven't touched the cabin at all!" exclaimed Aurore. It was a rare Yukon cabin that didn't have squirrels eating their spruce cones on your kitchen table the moment you left it.

The cabin had three rooms plus an extra long roof on the front to make the usual Yukon cabin porch. There were lots of nails on the outside wall in the porch to hang your axes, traps and saws. The back room used to be the office and we decided it would be the bedroom. The middle room had the woodstove, so it became the kitchen and dining room. "We'll call the front room the 'salon' just like in a French palace," joked Papa. "You children can entertain us with songs and amusing stories every evening."

"Même s'il n'y avait aucuns écureuils dans la cabane, nous allons la nettoyer. Complètement," said Maman firmly. I sighed. Even if we moved into the Queen of England's palace Maman would make us clean it. Kip ran to get some water and I gathered kindling to light the fire.

I took the kindling into the kitchen and was about to open the woodstove when I saw something that made me gasp. "Maman!" I cried. Everyone ran into the kitchen. "Look at this!" I said. I pointed at a cast iron frying pan lying in front of the woodstove. "It looks like it's covered in blood!"

Maman was unimpressed. "Et alors?"

I stared at the pan. Was I the only one who could feel something? Something ... terrible?

Aurore sighed. "Come on, Papillon. You know how our family is. If it's dirty, clean it. And if it looks clean, clean it anyway."

I whispered to her. "Do you think it's the ghost's blood?"

"I don't know," she said with that bored sigh she uses whenever she thinks she's the only kid in the world with chores. "But you're cleaning it."

I quickly put the frying pan back on the floor and went to sweep the floors and wipe the wooden boxes Papa set up as tables. I had to sweep several times since Kip was up on the roof and kept knocking dirt onto the floor. It was a typical Yukon cabin, with a sod roof made of logs with dirt on top. Kip had to put new dirt on any spots where the sod had blown away or dried up. Every time he moved, small showers of dirt would fall between the logs in the ceiling.

Yves was running around inside, telling Kip where he could see light coming through the roof. Each time, Yves would stand underneath and shout the news to Kip.

"Right here?" Kip would say, banging his shovel on the roof and sending a shower of dirt onto Yves face.

After the third time, Yves realized Kip was doing this on purpose and went outside to gather left over firewood from the other cabins.

I was about to go help him, when Maman called me into the kitchen. She gave me a wire brush and told me to scrape the blood off the plank near the woodstove.

"Mais, Maman—"

"Ne sois pas bête, Papillon. C'est juste une poêle rouillé."

"It's just a rusty pan. It's just a rusty pan," I kept repeating to myself as I scraped the floor with the wire brush. It was hard to get the stain out. It had soaked into the wooden plank. I rubbed it hard, scratching the top layer of wood off with the stiff bristles. Little pieces of saw dust piled up until the stain was completely gone. In its place there was a patch of pale, fresh wood on the floor.

Then I grabbed the pan and, instead of cleaning it, I just threw it behind our woodpile. It was a relief to get it out of the house.

Finally, Kip was done on the roof and I swept the whole cabin one last time. The cabin *looked* much better. But somehow it didn't feel much better.

I helped Maman unpack the kitchen box. We hung our pans on nails in the wall and I hung my little bag in the bedroom. It had my book, my journal and the painting set I got for my birthday.

Then we had a quick dinner of baked beans and crackers. I asked Papa all about Hard Luck Henry's stories. "Is it true there's a hidden gold cache with a giant nugget shaped like a lucky eight?" I asked.

Papa laughed. "If Hard Luck Henry spent more time mining and less time listening to crazy stories he might have more luck!" He told us about the time Hard Luck Henry was out on his claim and he opened a box of frozen eggs. Inside, there was a note from a farm girl in Washington saying that she'd love to marry a real Sourdough. So Henry trekked to Whitehorse, went to Seattle, got a train and found the girl. "The problem was that she'd written messages on lots of boxes of eggs! And Hard Luck Henry's eggs were so old that by the time he read the note on the box of eggs in Dawson she was already married to another guy from Dawson City who also liked eggs. When Hard Luck Henry got there they were married and had twins!"[1]

We all laughed. "Is that true, Papa?" I asked.

"Likely as true as the rest of Hard Luck Henry's stories."

"Tell us more!" I said. I always say that when it's almost bed time.

Papa went on. "You know that Alastair Riveridge that Henry was telling you about? He was Rufus Slight's partner in the mine. They were old friends from way back and owned the mine together. They say Alastair was planning to ask somebody to marry him and was saving up his gold to get a house and all that. But then he disappeared one day. All they ever found was his canoe, stuck under a tree just below Miles Canyon and Devil's Punchbowl."

"Did he really have gold?"

"They say he did and that he hid it somewhere, probably around here since he was living here at the time. As for the Lucky Eight nugget, I think that just an old miner's tale." Papa was always telling us that miners were superstitious and believed in all kinds of strange luck about finding gold.

"But what is the Lucky Eight nugget?" asked Yves.

"Well," said Papa, "if you listen to the miners they'll tell you that it's a nugget as big as your fist. It's shaped like an eight. But not just any eight. The bottom loop of the eight is twice as big as the top loop. The miners say that means that the man who owns it will keep getting richer and richer as he digs down on his claim."

"That's so crazy they should tell it to kids in Sunday school!" exclaimed Kip.

"Kip!" snapped Papa. Kip wasn't allowed to joke about Sunday school anymore, not after the Sunday school teacher came over

---

1.   Editor's note: This story also appears in Robert Service's poem "The Ballad of Hard Luck Henry" published several years after Papillon's journal was written. It is possible the poet heard the story from Papillon or her friends during his years in Whitehorse, but this cannot be confirmed.

one night and complained to Papa that Kip kept asking what the force of gravity was in heaven.

Papa didn't know yet that Kip kept asking our science teacher the same question.

Anyway, Papa could sense one of Kip's jokes was on the way. So he cleared his throat, which always means he's trying to act stern. "Now get to bed everyone or I'll give you all Lucky Chore nuggets!"

We all giggled as we ran into the bedroom to find our pyjamas.

I helped Yves. He was very worried that mice would eat his Three Musketeers hat and tunic. That's an old-fashioned kind of shirt the musketeers used to wear. So I found a nail for him and banged it into the wall. He hung his wooden Three Musketeers sword, tunic and hat on it. "Perfect! Thanks big sister," he said with a hug.

"All for one and one for all!" I replied. That's what the Three Musketeers say to each other whenever they help each other out. Then Yves jumped onto the bed and crawled under Papa's giant sleeping robe.

"Not so fast!" said Papa with a smile as he came in. He unrolled his buffalo robe on the floor. "Parents in the bed and—" He paused as he reached under the sleeping robe and pulled out Yves. "Kids on the buffalo robe!"

We tossed our sleeping robes onto the buffalo robe. Maman hung a towel across the window to block out some of the midnight sun. Everyone was tired after a busy day and pretty soon I could hear the soothing breathing of five people asleep near me.

I lay there, sometimes watching a mosquito fly into the beams of midnight sun coming through the cracks in the wall, or maybe counting the logs on the ceiling. But mostly I wrote in my journal and wondered about the ghost.

It already seemed so long ago. Did I really see it or was it just fog? And what about Hard Luck Henry's story about the ghost? Was it really true?

I was still thinking the same questions as I woke up the next morning. "Just five more minutes," I said to myself and rolled over.

"Papillon!" shouted Aurore from the kitchen. "Maman told you to scrape up this stain!"

I jumped up and ran into the kitchen. The stain was still there! It was bright red and really did look like blood this time. Even worse, the old frying pan was back!

"But I really did clean it!" I said. I shivered as the hairs on the back of my neck bristled. That strange feeling was back again.

Maman sighed and signaled Kip to give me the wire brush.

Kip read the label on the handle with a laugh. "Mr. Good-Buy's Patent Wire Brush. Say 'Good-Buy' to your stains!"

"Thanks a lot," I replied as I grabbed the brush and everyone went back to their own chores.

I was really mad as I scraped the stain off again. It was harder this time since the red wasn't dried on and got all over the brush. I looked up to see if Kip and Yves were smirking at me. Maybe it was their joke. Then I went outside and put the frying pan in a new hiding spot, sliding it extra far under the cabin's porch.

Above: Our cabin at Canyon City.
You can see the flowers growing on the roof!

Journal #4

July 1st, 1902
Canyon City, Yukon Territory
By candlelight on our second night in the cabin

We spent most of the day unpacking and getting Papa's wood cutting gear ready. He has different kinds of axes for chopping trees down, for limbing them and for splitting firewood. Kip spent all morning sharpening them all.

There were also all kinds of saws, chains, spikes and equipment for the horses to pull the logs out of the forest.

At lunchtime, we all sat down by the river and threw rocks in the river while we ate our sandwiches.

It was a wonderful time, until we saw a canoe cruise by. "Watch out!" muttered Yves as he squinted across the river. "Here comes Red McGraw!"

Red McGraw was not a nice man. When Maman, Aurore and Yves were on the Chilkoot Pass they hired him as a porter to carry their food and supplies. They didn't know he was an outlaw. He waited until they were at the Golden Stairs, the steepest part of the trail, and then asked for more money. When Maman said no, he ran off with half of their food.

It turned out later that he used to be a sheriff in Alaska, except that he was the kind of Alaskan sheriff who also was a robber. He got caught after he blamed Black Moran for one of his robberies, but Black Moran was an even bigger villain and challenged him to a gunfight.[1]

It's stories from Alaska like these that make me thankful Sam Steele and the other North West Mounted Police came to the Yukon. During the gold rush, Sam Steele would just give bad guys like Red McGraw a "blue ticket" and make them leave the Yukon. If you were only a little bit bad, he would just make you chop firewood for the police for a few days.

That's why Kip says Maman reminds him of Sam Steele whenever she catches him doing something and sends him into the backyard to split wood for the fire.

I wished they could still give Red McGraw a blue ticket, but Papa already went to see the police and they said he hadn't broken any Canadian laws.

"Yet," is what I said when I heard that.

Anyway, Yves picked up a rock and threw it as hard as he could, but the canoe was too far away. Red McGraw tipped his hat to us in mock respect and laughed. Then he kept paddling.

"Is he working for Rufus Slight up the river now?" asked Papa with a frown.

Anyway, after lunch Papa gave us a long break. I got my painting set from the cabin and started painting Papa sawing a tree. It was beautiful with Grey Mountain in the background and lots of green trees all around. All I had left to paint was Papa's red plaid lumber-jack shirt when I discovered my red paint was missing!

---

1.   Editor's note: Papillon's version of this story is again strangely similar to "The Duel" by Robert Service, in which Black Moran challenges Sheriff Red McGraw in a saloon showdown. Black Moran also features in *Yukon Secret Agents*, which was published last year and is based on Kip Dutoit's adventures during the Alaska-Canada border dispute.

It was sure annoying to have to give him a green shirt. He hates green shirts.

That night we had a big dinner in the cabin. After dinner, we sat around the woodstove and talked. I had saved all the newspaper pages Maman had used to pack up our boxes. Kip and I sprawled out on the floor by the woodstove. It's fun to read old newspapers. One was five years old and was all the way from Vancouver. The others were from the Whitehorse Star.

"Hey! Look at this," I exclaimed. "This article is about Rufus Slight's mine striking it rich!"

"And this one has a poem called The Old Log Cabin," replied Kip. He stood up straight, looked at us all and cleared his throat. "Ladies and gentleman," he began in his best English accent. "Tonight it is my privilege to present a poem."

He read the poem. It was about how when you have all kinds of troubles, you always dream about that little old log cabin in the pines. You couldn't help thinking about our cabin. The part I remember went like this:

And he sees old Death a-grinning and he thinks upon his crimes,
 Then he's like to have a vision, as he settles down to die,
  Of the little old log cabin in the shadow of the pines.

When Kip was done we all clapped. "Bravo!" laughed Maman, even though she probably hadn't understood any of the poem.

"Who wrote it?" I asked.

"Some guy named Robert Service," answered Kip. "It says he lives in Victoria."

"Well, if he loves log cabins so much he should move to the Yukon!" I said.[2]

Papa clapped Kip on the shoulder. "Gather round everyone," he shouted. "Time for a buffalo robe show!" That's what we called it when we sat around the woodstove and sang or told stories. Papa loved a good story or song around the fire. He would often tell us stories he had heard in the bush, or from famous Yukon story tellers like Jack London. He said it was important to be able to tell a good story. "Just look at Jack London," he would say. "That tough winter on the Stewart River during the gold rush. He kept everyone's spirits up. They came from miles around to hear his stories!"

I took the first turn. I took off my socks and told a sock puppet story. My left sock was the princess and my right sock was the prince. I made Kip take of his socks to be the horse and the ogre.

"Great idea. They smell like ogres!" exclaimed Yves.

When I was done, Papa took a turn. "Tonight, I'll tell you the story of Mangled Mike and the Deadly Dredge—"

"No," I cried. I'm not scared to sing songs or tell sock puppet stories, but scary stories are too much! "We shouldn't tell ghost stories! Hard Luck Henry says this place is haunted."

But everyone else wanted to hear it so Papa went on. "You know what a dredge is? It's a giant boat with a huge engine inside. Its buckets scoop up tons of gravel and smash it and twist it and shake it to get the gold out. It has a long conveyor belt that just keeps going and going and going. It's powerful enough to rip whole trees out of the ground. You know what happens if you get your shirt caught in it?" He looked around. "Well, you've seen Maman feed moose meat into the grinder right ..." We all squirmed.

"Well this dredge was haunted. It had a mind of its own." At this point I clapped my hands over my ears. I only heard the ending, where Papa described poor Mangled Mike after he got pulled into

---

2.   Editor's Note: Robert Service did write a poem called "The Old Log Cabin" before he moved to the Yukon. He sent it to the Whitehorse Star where it appeared in May, 1902 about a month before Papillon's journal. Two years later Service moved to Whitehorse. He wrote the poetry that made him famous in 1906 and moved to Dawson City in 1908. Papillon's version of the poem is slightly different from the one published in Spell of the Yukon.

the dredge. "Gruesome" or "ghastly" is how Miss Conrad would have described it.

Everyone clapped. "My turn! My turn!" shouted Yves.

"Is it a ghost story?" I asked. He shook his head.

We all gathered around. "Closer, closer," said Yves. "You've got to be real close." He waited while we shuffled closer. "Before I begin, I'll need those socks Papillon had." He took Kip's socks and mine. "OK, so there was this family. They lived in a cabin in the forest."

His voice kept getting quieter and quieter and we all leaned in. "There were two brothers. The handsome younger one and the ugly older one. The older one wasn't very smart either. One night, the family was telling stories around the campfire."

His voice was so quiet we could hardly hear it. We all leaned closer. Yves went on. "Anyway, the smart younger brother got the ugly and thick-headed older brother to take off his socks ..." I could see Kip's eyebrows begin to rise. Yves quickly went on with his story. "... and once the ugly and thick-headed older brother had taken off his socks, the smarter younger brother grabbed his hat and ran out the door."

Before we could blink Yves was out the front door, laughing and waving Kip's hat in the air on the end of his wooden sword. Kip ran right after him and was soon yipping in pain as his bare feet hit the rocks outside the cabin.

We all laughed as Kip found his boots and hunted around for his wooden sword before chasing after Yves.

We all went out on the porch to watch. Sam Steele loved sword fighting and used to teach us all the tricks. "En garde," shouted Kip as he moved to attack. That's how you tell the other person to get ready. Musketeers never attack someone who's not ready.

"Thrust!" cried Kip as he jabbed at Yves.

"Parry!" laughed Yves as he used his sword to knock Kip's away.

They circled each other. Kip tried a feint, which is when you fake one way and go another. But Yves just laughed and jumped backwards a step.

"Bravo!" I cried.

Papa tapped me on the shoulder. "Watch this. See how Kip isn't attacking anymore? He's waiting for Yves to make a mistake."

Sure enough, Yves thought he had Kip on the run and swung his sword in a wild attack. Kip blocked it, then lunged forward where Yves was unprotected. "Gotcha!" he shouted.

Yves staggered backwards, pretending to be wounded before grabbing his sword and chasing after Kip again.

"They're pretty good," I said.

"They practice more than the musketeers ever did," laughed Papa.

Above: Some of Papa's friends running a scow through the White Horse rapids. Pretty scary!

Photo courtesy of MacBride Museum (1989-3-117)

Journal #5

July 2nd, 1902
Canyon City, Yukon Territory
Writing in the old police cabin just before dinner

Today wasn't very fun. First of all, we missed yesterday's Dominion Day parade in Whitehorse because we're stuck out here cutting wood. I'm not looking forward to hearing Lucy Ogilvie tell me about all the candy she got.

Knowing her luck, she'll probably end up going to the Fourth of July parade in Skagway and getting a load of American candy too.

Secondly, when I woke up this morning the stain was back in front of the woodstove. Even worse, the pan was there too.

"It's not funny," I told the family. But no one seemed to notice as they rushed around doing their own chores.

The day didn't get any better when we went out to help Papa with the wood cutting. It seemed to take forever carrying all the axes and saws to where Papa needed them. Then it was hours of stacking wood, moving brush and so on.

I was sure glad when it was quitting time and we started walking back to the cabin. My hands and arms were aching.

We were almost back to the cabin, when we saw two men on the other side of the river. "Red McGraw," muttered Aurore. She didn't point, but we could see who she meant. "The same ugly red plaid jacket as yesterday."

The other man stepped gingerly into a canoe. Red McGraw pushed it off into the river once the man was ready. It was clear he was going to ferry across the river to us, but it took a few tries for him to get the angle right.

"Hello, Mr. Slight!" shouted Papa with a wave to the man in the canoe, ignoring Red McGraw on the other side of the river.

The man just nodded. Either he was rude or his hands were busy with his paddle.

"A friend of Red McGraw's?" asked Aurore in mock politeness.

"Be polite, you rascals!" said Papa quietly. "Rufus Slight is a good customer."

"A good customer on the cash list!" replied Aurore. That meant that Papa always asked to be paid for the wood when he dropped it off. Not like when he sells wood to the police or Taylor & Drury's store. He trusts them enough to drop off the wood "on account." That means he gives them a bill and knows they will pay later. Aurore writes all the bills since Papa never went to school when he was a boy and Aurore doesn't approve of his spelling.

I wondered why Mr. Slight was on the cash list as I watched him land his canoe. As soon as the canoe touched, a giant black dog leaped onto the shore and waited for him to get out.

We all knew Mr. Slight from seeing him at church, but he never talked to kids. He always sat near the front. He sang extra loud and was always all kissy-kissy with the priest.

Mr. Slight followed his dog up the bank towards us. "Whoa Shadow!" he shouted. He grabbed the dog's collar and yanked Shadow sharply backwards until the dog sat down.

Then he shook Papa's hand and they started to talk like adults.

"Some weather, eh?" asked Papa.

"You bet. Better than 40–below," replied Mr. Slight. His lips pressed together in a sort of a smile.

You know. The same old jokes adults always tell to each other when they don't have anything useful to say.

But Mr. Slight didn't really smile. It was more like a grimace. It was as if he didn't really believe in joking with people but had memorized a few jokes because he knew he was supposed to.

Mr. Slight ignored us kids the whole time. I watched him, describing him to myself like Sam Steele had taught us. It's the best way to remember things.

Mr. Slight was much taller than Papa. He was also thin, although his arms looked strong. You would call him "wiry." His hands looked tough, which made me think he knew about work and machines. But his clothes were tidy and clean. He had a clean black shirt tucked into some clean work pants. His belt buckle had a big "8" on it. His hat was a fedora, more like a banker would wear in the big city rather than Papa's wool cap. It was new but had some dust on it, which reminded me he was a miner.

But the funny thing was his face. It was even skinnier than his body. Maybe that was why he always looked sort of pinched and unhappy. He had straight black hair that flopped over his eyes and he had a black moustache. Well, not really a moustache. More like a gang of hairs hoping to be a moustache when they grew up.

His dog Shadow sat beside him. Unlike Mr. Slight, he did pay attention to us. The same kind of attention a lynx pays to rabbits. When he saw me watching him, he flashed his teeth at me and snarled.

It was scary! I stepped backwards and behind Kip.

"It's just a dog," whispered Kip. "Don't be a scaredy-cat."

That made me upset. I knew it was just a dog. But there's something about dogs. And ghost stories. And mines and caves. Some things I'm just scared of. Not everything's as easy as climbing a tree or performing a sock puppet play for your class. "I'm not a scaredy-cat!" I retorted.

"Then go pet the dog," replied Kip.

I wanted to, but I just couldn't get my muscles to move. "It's too scary," I whispered. Kip pried my fingers off his arm and walked up to the dog. It didn't look happy. But it didn't bite him either. He patted it twice on the head. "See?" he said. He pulled my hand towards the dog, but I could see the dog looking at my arm. I yanked it back.

Papa didn't notice any of this. "Marie-Ange is making pike and potatoes," he said, using Maman's real name. "Why don't you join us for dinner?" Aurore rolled her eyes. A guest meant extra work and no jokes at the table. Yves opened his mouth to complain. He'll say almost anything in front of guests. I gave him a quick kick in the shins.

Mr. Slight looked down at us just in time to see Yves stick out his tongue and reach out to pinch me. Mr. Slight grimaced slightly as if deciding which was worse, kids or cooking his own dinner.

After a short pause he said yes. Maman's cooking is pretty famous.

We all sighed. There was no point in complaining now. Papa would just tell us that you didn't meet too many people in the Yukon bush, so having one over for dinner was a treat. Then he'd tell you about all the nights he spent alone at his old woodcutting cabin wishing he had someone to visit with. Then he'd send you to get more wood for the fire.

You know how fathers are.

Anyway, the dinner invitation seemed to put Mr. Slight in a better mood.

Papa sent Kip running ahead to tell Maman. I love watching Kip run. He can run forever. When he walks he looks awkward. But when he runs he looks as natural as a wolf.

Mr. Slight and the rest of us kept walking back to Canyon City. We rounded a corner on the trail and saw the old cabins. Ours was the only one with smoke coming out of the chimney.

Our cabin was definitely the best and it looked even better now that we had fixed it up a bit. Papa had planted some Yukon flowers onto the new dirt on the roof. Maman had put more in an old half-barrel by the front door. It was one of the few cabins with a wooden floor, and as we approached I could see Maman handing Kip the broom and pointing to the spots that he had missed in the morning.

Mr. Slight suddenly stopped. He pulled at his collar nervously and stared at the cabin. The little hairs pretending to be a moustache on his lip shivered for a second.

"What is it?" prompted Papa.

Mr. Slight twitched as if a cold drop of water had fallen off a leaf and gone right down the back of his neck. "Oh, err, nothing," he said, taking off his hat and putting it back on. "Just remembered something I forgot in town." He paused for a second. "That used to be my cabin before we moved across the river."

He didn't say it like he was mad at us for using it. He just said it.

Papa took it as a joke. "Well, you built it well. Three rooms for just six people! Pure luxury!"

Mr. Slight still seemed distracted. "I didn't build it. My partner did."

We were all quiet for a second. I remembered the sad story about Mr. Slight's partner Alastair disappearing in Miles Canyon and how they found nothing but his canoe stuck under a tree just below the Devil's Punchbowl.

We kept walking towards our cabin, but before we'd gone ten more feet the dog Shadow sat down. "Come on Shadow!" called Mr. Slight. But the dog didn't budge. It just stared at our cabin. Mr. Slight grabbed Shadow's collar and gave him a tug, but the dog dug his toes into the dirt and wouldn't move. "Stupid animal. He can stay there and starve," said Mr. Slight, whacking the dog with his work gloves.

The others carried on to our cabin, but I stayed and watched the dog. He wasn't interested in snarling at me anymore. He just sat there and stared, whimpering every now and then.

"I know how you feel," I said to myself. Then I pulled my journal out of my pocket and ran to the old police cabin, which is an excellent place to write your journal if you don't want to be bothered by any annoying family members.

Above: Some Yukon kids in a canoe with Mr.
Atherton from Taylor & Drury.

Photo courtesy of the Bill & Aline Taylor collection.

Journal #6

July 2nd, 1902
Canyon City, Yukon Territory
**Writing by candle in the middle of the night with everyone
else asleep**

I was late getting back for dinner. First I got in trouble for sneaking off
to write in my journal instead of setting the table and tidying the
front room. Then, even worse, the only chair left was right across
from Mr. Slight!

He was jumpy and irritable the whole time. It was like he couldn't
wait to leave.

I sat down and looked around. The cabin felt gloomy and dark.
Even the air seemed heavy.

"Where's my cheerful little sunshine fairy?" asked Papa. That's his
pet name for me.

"Waiting for the sun to come back," I said.

"But it's a beautiful day!" he replied. Then we looked out the window. Instead of the sun, dark black rain clouds were everywhere.

"That's strange," said Kip. His hand darted out to grab a potato.
Even faster, Papa grabbed his wrist.

"Mr. Slight is our guest. We'll let him say grace before dinner."

Mr. Slight seemed surprised. I was hoping he would say something funny like "Past the teeth and over the gums; look out stomach, here it comes." But he picked one of the usual graces. I like it since it reminds you to think about the needs of other people and not just your own dinner.

Maybe he wasn't so bad after all.

Mr. Slight cleared his throat. "Give us grateful hearts, O Father, for all thy mercies, and make us mindful of the needs of others, through Jesus Christ our Lord. Amen."

But before the rest of us could say "amen," the cabin was lit up by an angry stroke of lightning. A huge boom of thunder echoed across the valley. The clouds closed in and suddenly it was so dark that Papa sent me into the bedroom to get two candles.

Things got a bit better once Maman served the pike and potatoes. She cuts the pike into one inch blocks and then bakes it with blocks of potatoes and butter.

Everyone was very quiet at dinner. Not like usual. Maman tried to start the conversation.

"Kip, as-tu vu des animaux intéressants aujourd'hui?" She often would ask us if we'd seen any interesting flowers or animals to get the conversation started at dinner.

"Nope," said Kip, slouching in his chair and fiddling with his food. Maman raised her eyebrow. That's her signal that it's time to mind your P's and Q's. Kip quickly sat up straight. "Non, Maman," he said.

"Non, Maman," said Aurore.

"I saw two squirrels, a chipmunk, a whiskeyjack and a grouse," added Yves. He loved this kind of family activity.

Everyone looked at me. I decided not to mention the ghost. "I saw a white raven," I said.

Everyone laughed like I had told a joke. "It was right at the edge of Miles Canyon. It looked very old and wise." This made them laugh even more.

"There's no such thing as a white raven!" snorted Mr. Slight.

"There is!"

Mr. Slight laughed. "You don't really mean that do you?" He looked right at me. It was as if his eyes were burning mine.

I looked down. "No," I said.

"I didn't think so," he replied with a mean kind of laugh.

I didn't say anything for the rest of dinner. Why didn't I stand up to him? Why didn't I say something funny? "If there can be black dogs then why can't there be white ravens?" I could have said. Or why didn't I ask him if he didn't believe in animals he hadn't seen himself, like the elephant or the camel?

But I didn't. That made me feel even worse. I knew that Kip, Aurore or Yves all would have spoken up if they had seen a white raven. Why didn't I?

There was another long silence. Aurore began asking Mr. Slight about his cabin up the river. He said it was a few miles upstream. It was brand new and had a nice view of the river, with a fancy dog-house just outside the front door for Shadow.

"Why do you think your dog is so skittish at Canyon City?" asked Aurore.

Mr. Slight choked suddenly. "Excuse me. Just a tiny bone from the pike," he stuttered. Maman got him another glass of water.

Dinner ended not too long after that. After Mr. Slight left we cleaned up and went to bed. Maman and Papa were in the bed and the four kids were on Papa's buffalo robe on the floor. No one felt very good. It was as if the happiness in the cabin had poured out under the door and gloom had oozed out of the walls.

I had a bad dream. I dreamed I was a prisoner in a castle owned by Mr. Slight. Do you know what an "oubliette" is? The bad guy in the Three Musketeers, Cardinal Richelieu, uses them. They are secret dungeon rooms where you can put someone forever and forget about them. That's why they call them oubliettes, which is from the French word for "forget."

Anyway, I dreamed I was locked in an oubliette. My arms were wrapped in chains and I could hardly move. I tried to shake them off but every time I moved they just clanked more loudly and got tighter.

In my dream, I made one last try to get free. I used all my muscles to push against the chains.

My arm broke free! I felt my hand hit something soft and warm.

Suddenly, I was wide awake. So was Kip! My arm had been tangled in the blankets and had just hit him in the nose!

I could tell he was about to say something when suddenly we heard a chain clanking. We sat up.

"There it is again!" I said. This time it was as if chains were being dragged across the front room floor. Kip nodded and crept out from under the covers. He crawled over to the door to the front room and looked in.

"There's nothing there!" he said as he came back. Then, suddenly, there was a shriek.

"It's inside the cabin!" I gasped.

"No way," exclaimed Kip. He jumped to his feet, grabbed an axe-handle Papa was repairing and jumped into the front room.

Nothing happened.

Kip skipped back to the bed. He looked puzzled. "There was nothing there," he said. He crawled back under the covers. Within seconds, I could hear his deep snores again. But it took me a long time to get back to sleep.

The next morning, I was the last to wake up. Everyone else was standing in the front room beside the woodstove.

"Papillon! The blood's there again!" said Yves.

The frying pan was there too. I grabbed Mr. Good-Buy's Patent Wire Brush and kneeled down. The blood wasn't quite as red as the day before. In fact, it seemed a bit purple.

"I think we have a ghost," I said. Yves smirked annoyingly. Aurore rolled her eyes.

"I think we have a practical joker," replied Papa.

"But I heard chains clanking last night." Everyone laughed.

"Don't be ridiculous, little sister," said Aurore. Yves looked at me like I was making up stories.

"Kip heard them too!" I said. Everyone looked at Kip.

"Well, err, yes. I thought I heard chains too."

Suddenly everyone was talking. They all wondered what the noise was. Aurore thought it might be an old trap rattling in the wind as it hung on one of the cabins. Yves wondered if a fox had found an old sled-dog chain.

I felt a little tear in the corner of my eye. Kip was right beside me, munching on a pancake. He wasn't concerned at all, either about the chains or about whether anyone believed him. "Why do they believe you but never me?" I asked him.

"What?" he said. "You feel like that girl Cassandra in the stories? The girl who was always right but no one ever believed her?"

"Exactly," I replied. "But why won't they believe me?"

Kip thought about this for a minute. "Maybe it's because some-times it seems like you don't believe yourself either."

Then he spilled the coffee all over the table and everyone jumped up and started shouting and grabbing for tea towels. No one mentioned the chains again. Instead, everyone argued about those questions everyone argues about in the Yukon. Which kind of wood burns hotter? Pine or spruce? Why is it easier to split wood when it's forty below? Is it better to start a fire with the kindling piled like a teepee or criss-crossed?

I got up and went outside to sit on the porch by myself.

I could hear them all cleaning the table, when suddenly Yves piped up. "Hey, why didn't we notice that carving on the walls before?"

I ran back inside. On the wall of the front room, right beside the window, there were some words. The walls had lots of things carved or scrawled on them, like measurements and people's initials. But these weren't faded. Aurore walked over and read the words:

> Greed, grudge, hatred and envy,
> All these things can a friend be.
> They are the curse that traps me here
> Hidden in dark and frozen fear.
> Oh the key, love in a stranger's sight
> And knowing that Rufus Slight
> Has felt Hell's hot bite.

Above: Papa's friend Mike Cyr running a barge through the rapids.
Mike and his brother Tony Cyr piloted Jack London with Papa in 1898.

Photo courtesy of MacBride Museum (1989-28-3)

Journal #7

July 5th, 1902
Canyon City, Yukon Territory
Writing at tea time on top of a very big pile of wood

We settled into normal life for the next few days. Well, as normal as you can get when someone puts blood on the floor every morning, finds the frying pan no matter where you hide it and rattles chains at night!

The strange thing was that each morning the blood was a slightly different colour. It got more and more purple, then turned bluish and now was starting to get green.

I couldn't figure it out.

Not that I had much time. "We have to cut cordwood while the sun shines," Papa said every morning. I thought the saying was "make hay while the sun shines" but maybe it's different in the Yukon.

It is in our family anyway.

Every day, we would get up and do our morning chores while Maman made us breakfast. If you're getting bored reading about our chores, just think how we felt doing them. Gather kindling. Chop wood. Get water. Sweep the cabin. Wash clothes. Darn socks. Sharpen axes.

The only thing that made it fun was Kip and Yves constantly playing practical jokes on each other. It started with Kip. We all knew that sometimes he would sew your pant leg closed so you'd fall over when getting dressed. I watched as Yves checked his pants before putting them on.

But Yves wasn't ready for his sock to be sewed shut.

Boy, how we laughed as Yves hopped in circles around the room with his foot half in his sock!

Yves was still grumpy about it at breakfast. When Kip grabbed the plate with the last pancake on it, Yves crossed his arms and put on his sulky face.

"Anybody hear a noise last night?" Kip asked as he speared the pancake and dumped it on his plate. "Like chains rattling?"

I nodded. To my surprise, Papa nodded too. "Yes, you're right. Like a dream." He looked puzzled.

My little brother Yves pointed out the window. "Was it that chain out there?"

We all looked carefully. "What chain?" asked Kip.

"Just thought I saw one," replied Yves. "Pass the jam, please, Kip." Kip passed the jam, then looked down at his own plate. His pancake was gone.

His arm flashed out to grab Yves. But Yves was already on his feet. He dodged behind Maman's skirt, stuffing the pancake into his mouth. His brown eyes twinkled with delight.

We were still laughing as we picked up our lunch bags and followed Papa up the trail to work. Kip started telling us about how the Sourdoughs used to eat fireweed sandwiches when they ran low on food. I'd never heard that story before.

Anyway, we were soon at work. Papa and Kip would fell the trees. Then Aurore and I would limb them. That means chopping off the branches. You have to be careful doing that with the axe. You stand on one side of the tree to chop off the branches on the other side.

Then you switch sides. That way you never swing the axe on the same side of the tree as your feet.

You wear good boots just in case though!

Then Papa would tie them to one of our horses and drag them back to our big lumber pile. Then they were easy to cut into eight foot lengths and load onto Papa's cart for our horse to pull back to Whitehorse along the old tramway. Sometimes Papa would dump them in the river to float them back to Whitehorse. But a lot of them would get lost that way.

Yves had a job too. He was supposed to clear the brush, but he mostly just ran around and made jokes. He said his real job was to keep our morale up.

"I know what'll keep my morale up!" exclaimed Kip. "Lunch!" He winked at me and then opened the pack and handed us each our lunch from Maman. He grabbed his sandwich. "Yum! A double slice of ham today!" he said with relish.

As Kip chewed, I saw that he was watching Yves. Our little brother untied the handkerchief holding his lunch. I saw that Kip was folding up his lunch like he was getting ready to run. Then Yves held up his sandwich.

Sticking out from between the two slices of bread was a big pile of fireweed leaves!

This time it was Kip's turn to get chased!

We were all pretty sore and tired at the end of the day. As we walked back to the cabin. I wondered if maybe the blood stain and the frying pan were a practical joke.

I made Kip tell me if he was putting the blood there. He said he wasn't. I even made him do a double dog swear, which is pretty serious.

That night I hid the frying pan under the porch of the old police cabin. Kip watched behind me to make sure no one else saw where it was. Then, after everyone else was asleep, Kip put a chair with a pile of empty tin cans behind the front door. When he was back in the bedroom I closed the door and tied a piece of thread from the bedroom door handle to my big toe. That way, no one could get into the kitchen without us knowing.

There were more chain rattling noises at night, but as planned Kip and I pretended to be asleep. In the morning, a tug on my toe woke me up. Papa was trying to open the bedroom door.

I snipped the thread and squeezed past Papa. The front door still had the cans piled against it and no one else had left the bedroom.

We dashed into the kitchen. The pan and blood were back!

Kip and I stared in amazement. "What colour blood is that?" he asked.

I was puzzled. "It looks like French Aquamarine," I muttered. After Royal Red and Violent Vermillion, it's my favourite paint colour.

Just at that moment our horses Cardinal and Milady whinnied. I heard horse bells in the distance. It was two of Mr. Slight's men with four horses and a giant wood cart.

One of them was Red McGraw.

Papa went out to talk to them. I guess it's not polite for adults to say things like "I asked the police to arrest you but they couldn't prove anything." Red McGraw certainly didn't say "Sorry I stole your wife's food on the Chilkoot."

Instead they talked about the weather as Red McGraw rolled a huge wad of chewing tobacco and stuffed it into his cheek.

Finally, Red McGraw got to the point. "Mr. Slight sent us here to pick up a load of firewood."

"That's funny," Papa said. "I dropped off a load at his place in town a few weeks ago. That should do him till Christmas."

"Oh no," said Red McGraw's buddy. "We're supposed to pick up some firewood they're floating down the river from the mine. The pump's broken at the mine and it'll be two weeks till new parts arrive. In the meantime, Mr. Slight's got the whole crew cutting wood for the church contract. He says we might as well make him some money instead of sitting around looking at busted equipment!"

Just as he said that, we heard shouting on the river. There were a couple of men in a boat shouting as they tried to steer a huge raft of firewood logs.

Papa was surprised. I think Miss Conrad would have used the word "astonished."

"But I've got the church contract!" Papa exclaimed. "Father Pat always buys from me." The other man looked embarrassed. I don't think he knew that. But Red McGraw just smirked and spat some tobacco juice on the ground.

"Tell him what else," snorted Red McGraw, elbowing the other man.

"Err, Mr. Slight also told us to take some of the windows from his old cabin at Canyon City and build a nice porch for Father Pat on his house. You know, on the south side. Nice light for sitting on the porch, reading the Bible and all that." Papa frowned. The man went on. "You wouldn't, err, happen to know which cabin used to be Mr. Slight's around here would you?"

Papa was so surprised he didn't say anything for a second.

Red McGraw spat and smirked again. "I reckon it's that one," he chuckled, pointing at our cabin. I think he knew all along.

Papa left the men and went over to Maman. "C'est beaucoup d'argent, Marie-Ange. Beaucoup."

Our visitors didn't understand him, but I did of course. He meant that a lot of our family's money came from selling wood to the church.

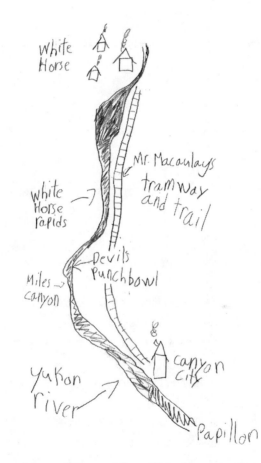

Above: A map of the trail from White Horse to Canyon City.
It's about six or seven miles long.

Journal #8

July 7th, 1902
Canyon City, Yukon Territory
Writing by candlelight in our bedroom just as the sun comes up

Papa went to town yesterday to talk to Father Pat. He didn't seem very optimistic, so Aurore and D'Artagnan went along with him to try to cheer him up.

We weren't very cheerful either, since Mr. Slight's men had taken our windows. I guess they weren't really our windows, but it felt like it. Maman covered one hole up with a board and another with a white sheet to keep the bugs out. The other we managed to replace with an old window that was sort of the same shape from another of the cabins.

We talked about Mr. Slight long into the evening. I thought it was rude of Mr. Slight to have dinner with us and then take our windows. "If that's not written in the Law of the Yukon, then it should be," I said.

Just as I said it, there was a rumble of thunder outside and a sudden gust of wind blew the willows against the walls of the cabin.

We sat around the fire again. Someone had stolen my painting set so I couldn't paint. Actually they just stole the paint and left the brushes, which is strange. So I just drew pictures of our cabin instead. Maman told us all about Mr. Slight, including the adult stuff she had never told before. I guess no one had ever really liked Mr. Slight in Whitehorse, especially not compared to his partner Alastair. Everyone enjoyed talking to Alastair. Maman said he was even more popular with the unmarried girls than a new police constable with a fancy red uniform.

It got surprisingly cold as she told the stories. Despite cuddling right up beside her, I felt the shivers several times and kept looking over my shoulder. I couldn't help feeling that someone was listening. Plus there seemed to be cold drafts everywhere. Kip had to relight the candles twice.

Maman told us that Alastair loved the rivers, so it was very sad when he disappeared in Miles Canyon. She said it was "ironic," which means it was the opposite of what you would expect.

There was an even stronger gust of wind when she said that. The willows scraped against the board over the window like fingers trying to get in.

"Maman," said Kip. "Is that how Mr. Slight ended up owning the whole mine?"

There was a sudden flash of lighting and more thunder. Strangely there was no rain. Maman looked up at the ceiling, then told us that it was just after Alastair disappeared that they found the paystreak at the mine. Before that, it never made much money. Alastair had picked the name Lucky Eight Mine, but it turned out that Mr. Slight was the one who got rich.

"Well, not as rich as the men in the Klondike who could buy their girlfriends enough champagne to have a bath in," observed Yves.

"But still pretty rich," said Kip. "Even richer if he really does have the Lucky Eight nugget."

"If it exists!" I added. "And if he's so rich, then why is he greedy enough to steal the church wood contract from us?" I asked. Maman shrugged her shoulders and blew out the candle.

Immediately we heard rattles and creaks from the cabin. "He's frisky tonight!" I thought. "I wonder what got him going?"

I cuddled in closer to Maman but she and Yves were already asleep. Kip was sprawled across the buffalo robe on the floor. I heard chains rattle, low moans and strange greenish lights under the door from the kitchen.

I buried my head under the covers. My eyes were as wide as they could get as I peeked out to watch the glow coming through the half-open door.

Then there was a particularly loud chain rattle. Kip woke up and pulled himself up onto one elbow.

His eyes widened as he saw the glow and heard the rattles and moans.

"Holy smokes!" he said quietly, looking at me.

But after a few minutes Kip began to look tired as the rattling and moaning went on and on. Finally, he yawned. "I need to get to bed. Papa'll kill me if that wood isn't cut up by the time he gets back."

I watched in amazement as Kip hopped silently out of bed and pushed open the door to the kitchen.

I was expecting a shriek or a scream, but instead we saw a strange glowing person flit silently by the doorway. He was carrying the frying pan!

I sat up to see more, but the door banged shut.

The next morning, the stain and the pan were waiting for us. The stain was still mostly French Aquamarine, but had a tinge of yellow near the edge.

It was all very strange. But at least Kip believed my story about the ghost. "How will we convince Maman?" he asked me the next day.

It was too bad Aurore wasn't there too. She was still in Whitehorse with Papa.

The next night, we heard the same noises. They were so loud that even Kip couldn't sleep.

"I don't mind sharing the cabin with a ghost," he said. "But the least he could do is oil his chains!"

The moans and chain rattling got louder. It seemed to go on for an hour. Suddenly Kip kicked off his covers and stood up. He flicked a match and lit a candle. Then he grabbed a bottle off the window sill and pushed open the door.

"No Kip!" I gasped. I was frozen with fear. I couldn't move a muscle as I watched him take a slow step into the room.

He paused for a second. A pale green light reflected off his face.

I screamed, grabbed Maman's arm and buried my head into her shoulder. My scream woke up Yves, but Maman just sighed and rolled over. I don't know how mothers get so tired, but there was no way I could wake up Maman that night!

I was terrified. I gripped Maman's arm. My fingernails were biting into Maman's arm but she didn't even flinch. I looked up for a second. It was the same ghost I'd seen on the river. He even had the same moustache and hat! But now, instead of having a paddle in his hands he was wearing a metal shackle around each wrist.

When he saw us, he turned and his eyes widened. There were bright red dots instead of pupils. His colour turned from flickering green to an icy sort of blue. He also rose higher off the floor and seemed to grow bigger. He leaned towards us, towering over Kip.

I tried to scream, but there was no breath in my lungs. All I could do was gasp. "No! No!" I croaked. Yves stared in shocked silence.

Kip cleared his throat. He looked a little nervous. But he stood up straight and looked the ghost in the eye, just like Maman tells us to do whenever we walk past the White Horse Hotel tavern, in case we meet our Member of Parliament. I squeezed Maman's arm a bit tighter.

"Mr. Ghost," said Kip solemnly, "it's a pleasure to make your acquaintance. We don't mind you rattling around at night, but please oil your chains. Here's a bottle of Peabody's Original Super-Efficacious Machine Oil. It'll work real good."

The ghost stared first at Kip, then at me and then at the bottle of Peabody's Original Super-Efficacious Machine Oil. He seemed to shrink a bit and he glowed a bit less brightly.

Then he shrieked. Well, not really a shriek. More like a howl of annoyance.

The ghost turned bright red and dissolved into a pink glowing mist like the Northern Lights that gushed past us like a strong wind. Kip's candle blew out and we all flinched backwards.

I heard Kip strike another match. "Well, that was rude," he said. "I was just trying to help."

Journal #9

July 8th, 1902
Canyon City, Yukon Territory
Just before dinner, on our porch

The next morning we found the frying pan in its usual location but there was no stain.

"I guess we disturbed him," laughed Kip.

"I bet he'll be back tonight," replied Yves.

"Don't say that!" I said.

"I bet he'll be back tonight," said Yves again. "And we'll be ready for him, right Kip?" There was a twinkle in his eye.

I tried to stop Yves and Kip that evening, but it was impossible. They searched all over the cabin until they found the ghost's chain. It was hidden behind the woodstove under the firewood box.

"Peabody's Original Super-Efficacious Machine Oil, please," said Kip in mock seriousness.

"As requested, sir," said Yves, slapping it into his hand.

Kip quickly oiled the chain and put it back in its spot.

That night, probably around midnight, we were woken up by the usual creaking and squeaking followed by some ghostly moans. Then we heard a scraping noise in the kitchen.

"He's lifting up the firewood box to get his chain!" whispered Kip.

"Get ready," said Yves.

"Ready for what?" I asked, jumping into bed with Maman and hiding under the blankets.

Then we heard it. Metal clicking together, first slowly then more frantically. Kip giggled. "No more noise than a well-oiled bicycle chain!"

We heard an annoyed shriek and the chain fell to the floor. Slowly our door creaked open and an eerie green glow flooded our room. I was frozen to my spot, eyes wide open, as the ghost stepped into the room. His red eyes flashed and he raised his arms over his head like an enraged grizzly bear.

"Get him!" hissed Kip. Suddenly my brothers pulled out their peashooters. "Pfft" went Kip's and the pea bounced off the ghost's forehead. Then Yves fired. Two peas flew out, one hitting the ghost in the nose and the other in the left eye.

"Double whammy!" shouted Yves triumphantly.

The ghost's hand clapped down over his left eye and he stumbled backwards, slamming the door as he went.

Kip and Yves shook hands. "We'll have to thank Mr. Galpin at school. We never would have learned to be such good shots without getting so much practice in Latin class."

The next morning the boys jumped out of bed. The pan was in its usual place but there was only a wet mark by the stove. "He only used water instead of blood," said Yves. "Pretty sad."

"I'm not sure it's wise to taunt a ghost like this, you guys," I said to them. But they were already plotting for the next night.

I spent the day feeding the horses and brushing them and getting ready for Papa's return. My brothers were supposed to be cutting wood, but they spent most of the day having foxtail wars. That's where you pull a clump of foxtails out of the ground, then throw it at your friend. The roots hold the dirt into a perfect dirtball, and the foxtails make it easy to throw. It's a game only Kip and Yves could spend four hours playing.

Anyway, I was very worried as we got into bed. Kip and Yves had spent hours getting the kitchen ready. But what was the ghost going to do tonight, I wondered?

Maman fell asleep right away, but I could tell the boys were only pretending to be asleep.

About midnight, we heard more noises. The ghost tried the chain again. Peabody's Original Super-Efficacious Machine Oil was still working its wonders. The chain dropped to the floor. We heard the frying pan slide onto the floor too. Then we heard a strange voice. It was high-pitched and sounded half-strangled. "Tonight," it wavered, "the blood by the stove will be yours!"

I grabbed Maman's arm, but she just sighed and rolled over. I froze.

The door slid open and footsteps approached.

But it wasn't our ghost! This one was covered in bloody gashes and was holding what was left of his head in his left hand. I screamed. "It's Mangled Mike from the Deadly Dredge!" His left eye flashed red, while a bloody metal bar was stuck in his right eye just like in the story! The ghost stood in the doorway. The head laughed. The jagged metal in its eye bobbed around as its other eyeball looked at us.

It took another step forward. Even Kip looked worried.

The ghost pushed open the door. Suddenly a bucket of water that had been balancing on the door tumbled onto the ghost's head!

Or rather, where its head would have been if it still had one.

Water splashed everywhere. "Direct hit!" shouted Kip. He pulled out his peashooter and let fly.

The ghost turned and tried to run. Yves reached down and yanked a rope. As he pulled, the other end that had been lying unnoticed on the kitchen floor suddenly went tight just as the ghost's foot was stepping into it.

The ghost tripped heavily onto the floor. "Fruitcakes!" exclaimed his head as it bounced out of his hands and rolled into the corner.

"Attack!" shouted Yves. My two brothers jumped out of bed and grabbed foxtails out of a bucket by the bed. The ghost staggered around in the kitchen feeling for his head as a swarm of flying foxtail bombs burst all around him.

Finally, he found his head, stuck it on and ran out the door on the far side of the kitchen. One final dirtbomb from Kip hit him in the back just before we heard a "poof" and he disappeared.

Kip and Yves hopped up and down hugging and shaking hands and laughing. That is, until they noticed that Maman had woken up. Her icy stare froze them instantly.

"Dirtbombs dans la maison?" I knew she was mad since she never uses English words unless she's distracted.

She stuck out her hand, pointed at them, and curled her finger back to summon the boys. When they got close enough, she reached up and grabbed one of their ears in each hand. Then she pulled them closer until they were looking right at her from about two inches away.

"Grounded!" she barked in English. "Vous allez nettoyer toute la cabane demain!" she said, pointing at the broom they'd be using to clean up the mess the next day.

Then she sent them back to bed. "Now that was scary!" I heard Yves whisper as he crawled under his sleeping robe.

Above: The White Horse rapids are pretty dangerous in a canoe!
Photo courtesy of MacBride Museum (1989-4-772)

Journal #10

July 9th, 1902
Canyon City, Yukon Territory
After midnight on the bank of the Yukon River

It took Kip and Yves most of the morning to clean up the cabin. Despite their punishment, that night Kip and Yves secretly prepared for the next battle with the ghost. Maman was now watching them suspiciously. In fact, I think she may have been on the ghost's side.

I certainly was. "I think he's actually a nice ghost," I said. "I've never seen him hurt anyone."

Kip wasn't having any of it. "He came into our room pretending to be Mangled Mike from the Deadly Dredge! His head had a metal bar right through it!"

We all tried to stay up to see what would happen next. But nothing happened. Midnight came and went. A few coyotes howled in a bored sort of way across the river. It wasn't windy at all.

Finally, I fell asleep. I was woken a few hours after midnight by a noise in the kitchen. Kip, Yves and Maman were all asleep. It was like the ghost was sneaking around. I very quietly got out of bed and looked under the door.

There was a pale glow from the ghost's skin. He was on his tiptoes and was wearing moccasins wrapped in cloth. He stepped very gingerly towards the shelf, took the frying pan and very quietly laid it by the stove. Then he took a cup of water out from behind a log near the stove, mixed in some ashes from the stove, and poured a few drops onto the floor.

I was pretty scared. But he looked sad. I took a breath—a very deep breath—and pushed open the door.

The ghost jumped like I'd zapped him with an electric wire. He looked at me in terror and disappeared into a cloud of mist.

Kip and Yves were quite disappointed that the ghost had started sneaking around. "That's so unoriginal!" said Yves as we looked at the frying pan. "Water and ashes instead of blood?" Kip shook his head.

Later that day, Hard Luck Henry came up the trail from White-horse on his way back to his gold claim. Behind him were Red McGraw and a few of Mr. Slight's men going up to the mine to help with the next big load of logs.

Hard Luck Henry walked up to our door as Mr. Slight's men headed for the river. He had a note from Papa. Well, actually it was written by Aurore.

July 8th, 1902
Whitehorse, Yukon Territory

Marie-Ange Dutoit
Canyon City, Yukon Territory

Dear Maman,

I hope this letter finds you well. Papa asks me to write to tell you that he is detained on important business with the bank man-ager and will have to stay in town for two more days.

I am helping Mr. Drury in the stationery department at his store.

D'Artagnan is in good spirits.

Please give our love to Kip, Yves and Papillon.

With all due respect,
Your loving daughter Aurore

"It's like getting a letter from the Queen," Kip observed.

Then I translated it for Maman. She was quite worried about the words "bank manager." She wouldn't admit that she was worried, but I think it had something to do with Papa losing the church wood contract.

"Est-ce que nous avons besoin de l'argent?" I asked.

"Comme toujours," she said, giving me a hug. "Peut-etre pire que toujours."

I knew I had guessed right. We always needed money, but now we needed it more than ever.

Kip said he wasn't worried. "Yeah, I've heard Maman and Papa talking about that. But I'm not worried."

"Why not?" I asked.

"Because then we'd live at Canyon City year round and I wouldn't have to go to school!"

He and Yves laughed as if that would be the best thing ever. But I knew they didn't really think that.

That night we all went to bed early. It was almost like a normal night. For small talk, instead of saying "Do you think it will rain tonight?" we would just say "Do you think the ghost will be quiet tonight?"

Just after midnight, however, I was woken up. But it wasn't by the ghost. Instead, I heard the door creak as Kip slipped out of the bedroom. I saw that he was wearing his socks and had his boots in his hands.

I gave him a ten second head start then slipped out after him.

He entered the kitchen, took a quick look around for the ghost, then quietly opened the front door of the cabin. I watched him put on his boots and run quietly down to the riverbank. In my bare feet, I moved noiselessly behind him.

He was untying the canoe.

"What are you doing?" I hissed. I smiled as he almost jumped out of his pants in fright.

"Gosh!" he said. "You're scarier than any ghost."

"What are you doing?" I repeated.

"None of your beeswax," he said with a smile. "And if you tell Maman …"

"I won't." But I was scared. I grabbed his arm. "Promise me you won't canoe through Miles Canyon! The rapids are too dangerous!"

He hugged me. We could both hear the roar of the deadly waves in Miles Canyon. "Don't worry. I'm just ferrying to the other side."

I watched as he jumped into the canoe. He pointed it diagonally upstream and paddled. He was a very good canoeist. He paddled just enough to keep himself from slipping downstream towards Miles Canyon, but since the canoe was at an angle each stroke took him a bit closer to the other side.

There were clouds blocking most of the midnight sun, so I could hardly see him as he arrived on the other side and disappeared into the forest.

Journal #11

July 9th, 1902
Canyon City, Yukon Territory
Breakfast time, back safely in our cabin

I don't know how long I sat on the riverbank thinking about things. I leaned up against a tree and pulled my sweater around me. I think I might have fallen asleep a couple of times. One time, I felt like I was in a dream. I watched the mist pour down the river. Suddenly, just like on our first morning at Canyon City, I saw the mist pull together into a big shape.

As it got closer, I could see it was a canoe. And, sure enough, there was our ghost sitting in the middle! His paddle flashed twice to correct his line on the river, then he waved his hat in the air and shouted "yippee" before he paddled like mad and disappeared into the foaming rapids.

I was awake now. I noticed how the moon had moved through the clouds. Quite a bit of time had passed. How much longer would Kip be, I wondered?

Just then, I heard a footstep from downriver. I froze perfectly still. Then I heard another. It was the ghost! He was walking up the trail from the Devil's Punchbowl.

He glowed ever so softly in the moonlight. And he had a smile on his face!

He walked right past me, dripping water with each step as he walked towards our cabin.

Once he had gone by, I rose silently to my feet. Looking out for noisy sticks or rocks, I followed after him.

I think he heard me once, because he suddenly stopped. I crouched down instantly among the foxtails and fireweed. He looked around curiously, then turned and continued. I followed him as he stepped lightly onto the porch of our cabin.

Instead of opening the door, he passed right through it!

In two quick skips I was up to the window in the front room. I was just in time to see him glow a bit more brightly, then dissolve into mist. I was about to look away, when I noticed the mist swirling. One of the boards in our floor bent sideways like it was made of rubber. The ghost's mist swirled right through the gap.

I dropped to my knees immediately and looked around the bottom log of our cabin hoping to see the ghost come out somewhere.

What I noticed, though, was even more amazing than that. Through a tiny crack under the bottom log of the cabin, I saw a faint glow. I pressed my eye to it and saw the ghost again. Under our cabin!

I looked again, but he was gone and it was black.

I walked slowly back to the riverbank. There was no way I could go back to sleep now! I had seen the ghost again! Even more importantly, something else began to sink in. I had been right the whole time! I saw the ghost that first morning. It really existed even though everyone else made jokes about it. Even more, it lived right under our cabin and I'd been right about the frying pan and blood right from the beginning.

I was still thinking about this as the first sun appeared over the top of Grey Mountain. I saw the light flash onto the sandy hills along the river.

The air was crisp and pure. I felt like I could see forever.

In fact, far away up river I really could see something in the water. No! Many things. They were floating towards me as fast as the river could bring them. I edged towards the bank. A few minutes later they washed by me.

They were logs! Dozens—no hundreds of logs! All cut into eight foot lengths like firewood. They jostled down the river and disappeared into the roar of Miles Canyon, where the Yukon River tossed those heavy logs up in the air like they were toothpicks.

It was magnificent. That's the word Miss Conrad always uses when she looks at the Yukon River.

The last logs were still pouring by me. It might be magnificent, but it was also puzzling. Who would let so many logs go so early in the morning? And especially on a Sunday when it wasn't likely anyone would have their lumber crew working.

I looked up river again. Far, far away, on the farthest possible hill, I could see the wind gently blowing the grasses on either side of the trail. Then, without a noise, I saw something come out of the forest.

It was moving fast down the trail.

It was Kip! He was running with that beautiful stride I love to watch. His back was straight and his head was thrown back as if to catch more of the sunlight. Each stride seemed to bring him a mile closer to me. I could soon see that he had taken his shirt off and had it clenched in this right hand.

He ran on and on without slowing. Every once in a while he would wipe his brow with his shirt.

And once, when the trail went down low near the water, he stopped and crouched by the side of the river. He tilted his head as if listening for something, then looked over his shoulder. He suddenly became tense. He quickly dipped his hands into the river, took a drink and leaped to his feet and ran on.

He came closer and closer. The trail took him down low near the river. Suddenly, back where he first came into view, a man on a horse burst out of the forest. There was a black dog at his heels. I knew it was Mr. Slight. He raised his whip and slapped it onto the horse's flank. The horse leaped forward along the trail.

Suddenly, I was scared. Mr. Slight was riding like he meant business. I worried whether he could see Kip on the trail from where he was.

I ran down to the edge of the river and watched Kip burst out of the forest. He jumped into the canoe and ferried it quickly across.

"Hurry!" I hissed as he got close to shore.

"Run Papillon! They're after me!" he said. He tossed me the rope from the canoe.

I grabbed it and pointed upstream. From where we were standing, you couldn't see the trail on the other side. "They can't see you from here because of how the river curves."

Kip looked up the river and smiled. "Brilliant, Papillon. Thanks!"

He was about to jump out of the canoe when he suddenly stopped. He quickly unlaced his boots before jumping onto shore. I tied up the canoe as he ran to the cabin in his socks and slipped inside.

Mr. Slight burst out of the bushes on the other side of the river a few seconds later. He flipped his horse's reins around a tree and jumped into the other canoe. He wasn't quite as good as Kip, so it took him a bit longer to get across.

He stormed up the bank. "Your father's done it this time!" he said cruelly.

"Papa?" I said, in my dumbest kid voice. "He's been in town a week! I was just picking some flowers to make a bouquet in case he comes today."

Mr. Slight stopped for a second. "In town?"

"Yes. He's visiting the bank manager."

"Oh right." Mr. Slight looked flummoxed. He looked back across the bank, then in the mud at all the tracks. I realized why Kip had taken his boots off. "Did you see—"

"A man running?"

"Yes!" exclaimed Mr. Slight.

"Yeah," I said in my most bored voice. "He jumped in a canoe and went into Miles Canyon." Mr. Slight looked hard at me for a second. I guess he believed me because he threw his hat down on the ground and swore. I decided to have some fun with him. "He shouted 'yippee!'" I said. "Then he waved his hat in the air as he disappeared into Miles Canyon."

Mr. Slight froze for a second. He didn't look happy at all. He glanced up at our cabin in a nervous sort of way. Then he stomped back to his canoe and re-crossed the river.

I took my flowers up to the house and gave them to Maman.

"Des fleurs!" she exclaimed. Then Kip appeared out of the bedroom. He was wearing his pyjamas and pretending to be sleepy. He gave me a hug and offered to set the table for me.

Maman smiled and patted him on the head.

As he put my plate down in front of me, I smiled. Only I noticed that his socks were filthy and that he put his pyjama bottoms on backwards when he sneaked back into bed!

Journal #12

July 10th, 1902
Canyon City, Yukon Territory
Three hours past bedtime, on the tramway trail

A bit later that day, we saw Mr. Slight's men arrive on the riverbank. They were gathering any logs they could find that had got stuck along the bank.

Maman laughed and shook her head. "Lui vendre notre grange! Imaginez!"

"Maman," said Kip, speaking French. "I thought you said we shouldn't laugh at other people's misfortunes?"

Maman looked a bit embarrassed. "Tu as raison," she replied. Kip smiled like an angel and asked for more jam for his pancakes.

I wondered what Maman meant about Mr. Slight trying to make us sell him our barn back in Whitehorse. So I waited until she had made her morning tea and sat down beside her. I knew she didn't like to tell secrets about money to the kids.

So I decided to interrogate her. That's a word I learned when I helped myself to Kip's new Sherlock Holmes book. Sam Steele had brought it back for Kip from London on his last trip. It's about a detective who solves mysteries, and he always has to ask lots of questions. Except he uses the word "interrogate" which sounds much fancier.

So first I asked her whether she thought it would rain. Then about whether it would be windy. That was to get her comfortable answering questions. You can't just blurt out questions like "Why is Mr. Slight trying to buy our barn, and if he is, how can he make us sell it if we don't want to?"

Finally, I got to the point. It took a bunch of questions, but finally she told me that our barn was in between two of Mr. Slight's pieces of land back in town. If he got it, he would own the whole block and all his land would be worth even more.

"But how can he make us sell?"

"Papillon!" Maman laughed. "C'est comme la Bastille!"

I smiled. That's where Cardinal Richelieu in the Three Musketeers used to interrogate his prisoners, except that he tortured them with red-hot pokers.

I didn't have any red-hot pokers, so I smiled and batted my eyes as cute as I could and said please.

It worked. Maman told me that we owed the bank a lot of money. Papa thought Mr. Slight had told the bank manager about how Papa had lost the church wood contract. And since the bank manager would get in trouble if we didn't pay back the bank, he was asking for our money back now.

I understood right away. The only way we could get enough money was to sell the barn!

Maman sent me to play outside. She said she likes to drink her tea in peace, whatever that means.

I ran off and told Kip. "Oooh! That would be bad." Papa needed a barn for the horses in the winter and for all his equipment. He would have to buy new land somewhere else and build a new barn. "And while he was doing that he couldn't cut wood or earn money!"

We both sat silently for a moment and watched the river go by.

Then Kip smiled at me. "That's why I cut Mr. Slight's lumber loose last night!" Then he told me all about his night. He had run up the river trail to see how far away Mr. Slight's mine was. The mine itself was up the hills, but Kip found his camp where he had his cabin and supplies. It was right on the bank of the river.

"I thought I would just have a look around and see what was going on. You know, in case I wanted to get back some time and do something," he told me. "But then I saw the rafts of logs, with even more logs piled up on the dock. I found an axe and chopped as many ropes as I could find. I was pretty quiet and I don't think anyone heard me. Then I got a long pole and pushed the logs on the dock. Once one broke loose, the whole pile went! It was unbelievably loud! I tossed the axe into the river and took off along the trail. I heard all kinds of shouting and barking."

"How did you get away?"

"They came after me on foot first, but I was too fast. They had to go back and saddle their horses. I don't think they even saw me. I think they were following my tracks."

"I bet it was that dog Shadow," I said.

Kip nodded. "I know. That dog scares me."

"Me too. You know, Kip, what you did was very exciting but it doesn't actually help Papa pay off the bank."

That made Kip think. He sat silently on the riverbank and tossed tiny rocks into the water. I was thinking too. I just couldn't think of a way to help Maman and Papa!

Just then, we heard hooves. It was Papa and Aurore and they had brought ponies for all of us!

Papa swept me up in his arms and gave me a big hug. Yves came running out of the cabin and jumped on his back. Kip grabbed Aurore's hat and threw it in a tree. You know how boys are.

"I'm here to pick you all up," said Papa. "We've got to go back to town." It turned out that Papa was going to sell his barn.

It was sad, but we packed our things and tidied up the cabin. We put our things on our two big workhorses. But just before Papa closed up the front door of the cabin, I ran back inside. I don't know if he heard me, but I quietly said goodbye to the ghost.

Then I jumped on my pony. I had ridden him lots before. His name was Esprit and he belonged to a friend of Papa's.

We rode along the old tramway trail back to Whitehorse. It was easy riding, since tramways are always flat and straight. And it was a beautiful day.

But it was sad leaving the cabin at Canyon City. Especially since you could tell Papa was upset about the bad news about his barn. And somehow I felt sad about the ghost. I was always scared when he was there, but still it was sad leaving without finding out his story. Or maybe even talking to him.

We stopped for lunch halfway and Papa let us play on the sandy hills near the river. It was fun, but it meant we got back late to Whitehorse. "We'll camp here," said Papa, "and we'll get someone to ferry us across the river tomorrow." It was funny looking at Whitehorse from across the river. I was so used to looking the other way.

Papa unrolled his canvas tent and we all piled inside. Everyone else fell asleep in no time, but I couldn't.

I just lay there wondering how I could help Papa. But I just couldn't think of anything.

Then I had it! The ghost was Alastair, so I'd ask him where the Lucky Eight nugget was!

I crawled out of my sleeping robe and slipped under the flaps of the tent.

I stood by the river, thinking. If I told everyone my idea, they would laugh. No one would believe me. They definitely wouldn't ride all the way back to Canyon City to ask a ghost a question!

But I knew the ghost was there. And somehow, I knew I could talk to him. But if I waited until the next time we were at Canyon City it would be too late. Mr. Slight would already own Papa's barn and we could never get it back.

I thought about what Kip said when I talked to him about Cassandra. How no one believed me because I didn't seem to believe myself.

Suddenly, I knew what to do. I put the saddle on Esprit and put a bottle of water and some food in my bag.

What I did next seemed like the biggest thing I had ever done.

I stood beside Esprit with one foot in the stirrup for a long time.

Then I thought about what Kip said again. I kind of wanted to go back and cuddle in my sleeping robe with my family.

But instead I pulled myself into the saddle and whispered "Let's go!" into Esprit's ear.

Journal #13

July 11th, 1902
Canyon City, Yukon Territory
Back at Canyon City, some time after midnight

I rode hard to get back to Canyon City by midnight to see the ghost.

But it seemed much farther when I was alone. Every shadow seemed to be a wolf and I could hear the coyotes in the distance.

It was one of those beautiful Yukon summer nights as I left our camp near Whitehorse. But as I rode along, it seemed to get darker and windier. There were big black clouds in the sky like I'd never seen before in the Yukon.

In the distance, from behind Grey Mountain, I could hear thunder but I couldn't see any lightning.

When I got to the last corner before Canyon City, I saw a raven in the tree. It was a big black one, and it squinted at me for a moment as I stopped to look at it. Then it stretched out its neck at me and gave three unfriendly caws. Then it made a horrible noise and jumped into the air and flew right at my head!

"Aaah!" I screamed and Esprit skittered backwards.

Just then, out of nowhere, the white raven flashed out of the sky and dived in front of the black one. There was a terrible noise as they squabbled like ravens do.

Then there was silence as the black one disappeared into the forest.

"Steady," I said to Esprit as I rubbed her neck. Esprit didn't like that black raven at all. Neither did I. I wondered if it was a bad omen. That's something that signals bad luck is coming.

On the other hand, the black raven was gone and the old white raven was sitting on a branch looking right at me.

I shook my head. How could ravens know what was going to happen? On the other hand, if there were ghosts maybe ravens had some magic too.

I looked up at the white raven in the tree. I remembered how he had landed beside me the first time I saw the ghost. He tilted his head and looked at me. It was as if he was saying, "Well, what are you waiting for?"

I tapped Esprit with the reins. I rode as fast as I could towards Canyon City and our cabin. Or, rather, the ghost's cabin.

When I got there, I jumped off Esprit and tied the reins to a tree. Then I opened the front door and slipped into the front room. It was quite dark, since it had been getting cloudier as I rode along. I crawled along the floor where I'd seen the ghost disappear. There had to be something down there.

I ran my fingers along the edge of the floor. Then I noticed something! Two of the big planks didn't have any nails in them! I crawled quickly to the other end. There were no nails there either! I quietly moved two old chairs and a bucket off those planks. Then I squeezed my little finger down one of the cracks and pulled.

I could feel the plank move, but I couldn't quite get it. So I grabbed the woodstove poker and slid it into the hole.

There was another boom of thunder and a strong gust of wind hit the cabin, sending a chilly draft across the floor. The willows smacked into the window like a hundred bony fingers.

I shivered and looked back down at the board. Then I twisted the poker and pulled it up!

The board came right up in my hand. The smell of a hundred musty old suitcases came up out of a dark hole under the floor.

It was a secret room!

I quickly pulled up the other board. In the dim light coming into the cabin I could see the top rung of a ladder, but the rest was completely dark.

"I need a candle!" I whispered to myself. Then I realized I had forgotten to bring any. And Maman probably packed everything up before she left.

I dashed into the kitchen to check. There, in the middle of the table, were two candles and some matches. I remembered that we always leave a few spares whenever we leave a cabin. Just in case the next person forgets theirs.

"It's the Law of the Yukon," I said to myself with a smile. I grabbed the matches and a candle and ran back to the front room.

I lit the candle, stuffed the matches in my pocket and put my foot on the top of the ladder.

That was easy.

The second rung was not!

A million thoughts went through my head. What was down there? A ghost? Demons? The bones of kids who had snuck down there before?

I held out the candle, but the candleholder was blocking all the light going down. I tipped it sideways, but the candle almost fell out.

There was nothing else to do! I gulped and took another step down. "Hello, Alastair?" I said uncertainly.

I took another step. The ladder was rickety and I could only hang on with one hand since the other was holding the candle. I wished it wasn't so dark down there. I took a breath and then another step.

I put my next foot down. There was something on the rung, but I couldn't see it. I tried to push it out of the way with my foot.

"Yikes!" I cried as my hand suddenly slipped. I fell off the ladder and landed with a crash. I sat up. It was pitch black. I still had the candle holder in my left hand but the candle had bounced somewhere and gone out.

You can imagine how scared I was. I felt around on the floor for the candle. All I felt was dirt. What would I feel next? A candle? A chain? A bone?

My hand touched something cold. Very cold.

I pulled it back.

Then I remembered the matches. I put my hand in my pocket and pulled out the box of matches. Very slowly, in the dark, I pulled out a match and struck it.

I saw the candle, lying right beside my foot. I lit it and stuck it back into the candle holder.

Then, very carefully, I held up the candle and looked around.

At the bottom of the ladder were some old boxes of eggs and potatoes. I was in a root cellar! Beside the ladder were some small shelves that had an old pair of boots and some dusty long underwear hanging on them.

I slowly moved the candle around the root cellar.

Then, right behind me, I noticed a block of wood. On top of it was a plate, a little tin pitcher and a glass. The plate was covered with three round, moldy shapes. The little pitcher had something black inside and the glass was full of whitish, crusty stuff.

I looked at them for a moment. "Pancakes, milk and syrup!" I gasped.

A horrible feeling came over me.

I lifted the candle higher and looked behind the wooden block.

Then I saw him! There was a skeleton lying face down on the floor. It's hands were reaching out for the pancakes, but there were chains on its wrists that went back to enormous spikes driven into the log walls.

A tear came to my eye. "Oh Alastair!" I sighed sadly.

Journal #14

July 11th, 1902
Canyon City, Yukon Territory
Beside the Yukon River, some time after midnight

I sat back on the floor and looked at Alastair's skeleton. Who did this?

And, more importantly, why hadn't I seen his ghost yet?

I was just wondering this when I heard a footstep on the porch. I quickly blew out my candle and looked up. There was a glow filling the front room above me.

Soon I saw the glowing mist sweep down through the cracks in the floor and reassemble into the shape of a man!

He was sitting on a chunk of firewood across the root cellar from me, looking down at his skeleton.

A drop of water fell from his sleeve onto the floor.

He looked unbelievably sad.

"Why are you so sad?" I asked.

The ghost leaped to his feet in surprise and went "poof." I lit my candle again and looked around, but he was completely gone.

Oh well, I thought. That's more or less how I reacted the first time I saw him.

But then, slowly, the glowing mist came back and reformed again.

"You scared me, miss," said the ghost.

I stood up. "I'm called Papillon," I said. "It's a pleasure to make your acquaintance Alastair. I mean Mr. Riveridge."

He blinked at me. "Well that's a change. Usually people scream and run away in panic when they meet me."

"Well, of course they do, Mr. Riveridge. You sneak up on them at night dressed as Mangled Mike of the Deadly Dredge!"

The ghost sighed. "I guess that's true." He reached out to shake my hand but my hand went right through his. "Oh, err, sorry. I forgot about that." He seemed embarrassed.

"Don't worry," I replied. "It's not too spooky."

He smiled a little. "You can call me Alastair."

We sat down and looked at each other. He spoke first. "I don't really like sneaking up on people. But it's the Law of Ghosts."

"Sort of like the Law of the Yukon?"

"Exactly. A whole bunch of complicated stuff that cheechakos—I mean live people—don't understand. I have to haunt this cabin. Every night, I have to go upstairs and put the frying pan by the woodstove and check on my stain."

"Is paddling Miles Canyon in your ghost canoe part of it too?"

"No. I'm not really supposed to do that. Ghosts aren't supposed to have fun. But nobody checks up on me around here very much. In fact, most of the time there's no one to haunt. I just go upstairs and check on my frying pan every night. It's always in the same place, since no one ever comes here. Before you guys arrived, the most exciting thing I did was scare a squirrel. I didn't like the idea of squirrels eating spruce cones on my frying pan."

"That's why the cabin was so easy to clean!" I exclaimed. "But Alastair, why is the frying pan so important?"

A painful look came over his face. "That's what my friend—my best friend—Rufus Slight hit me with. Then he dragged me down here and chained me up."

I gasped. "So that stain ..."

He nodded. "Is my blood. Or at least it was, until you started scraping it up every morning. I got kind of mad at you kids. Why did you have to clean it up every day?"

"Maman made us clean it up. And I got mad at you! You used up all my paints that I got for my birthday. And who ever heard of blood coloured French Aquamarine anyway?"

He sighed and looked sad again. "I know. I know. But it's hard to find blood, and I can never remember how ghosts are supposed to make it. I'm not on top of all the ghost tricks. It took me forever to change myself into Mangled Mike. I know I'm not a very good ghost. I mean, I couldn't even frighten you away. And you're just a little girl. You're supposed to be the easiest to scare."

It was sad seeing him so depressed. "Yukon girls are a bit different," I said.

"Don't I know it! And Yukon boys too! I tried all my tricks on you guys. Your brothers just laughed in my face and shot me with peashooters and foxtail bombs! That doesn't happen to ghosts in Europe!"

Alastair sighed. He seemed sad. I sat quietly and waited for him to speak again.

"Why couldn't I really be like Mangled Mike? All he has to do is show up in a hotel hallway in Dawson City and everyone starts jumping out the windows. Or Sam McGee? Father Pat opened his woodstove one night and saw a miniature version of Sam McGee sitting right in the coals! He threw his whiskey right out the window!" Alastair sighed again. "I wish I could be more like them."

"You're a very good canoeist," I pointed out.

"Oh, that don't matter. That was just for fun."

"Everyone says you were very popular," I suggested.

That seemed to get him a bit excited. "I know! That's the problem. Everyone liked me because I had nice hair and nice teeth! I never succeeded at anything real. I started a restaurant back home. Everyone got sick, even Rufus. I got a job on the railway and forgot to attach the caboose!" He shook his head. "Boy, that was a mess." He got up and started pacing around the root cellar. Miss Conrad would have called him agitated. If he didn't scare the dye right out of her hair first, that is.

I waited silently. Alastair seemed to need someone to talk to. "And when Rufus and I got here, it kept happening. We were the slowest pair over the Chilkoot, but everyone liked me! When we got to Dawson, all the best creeks were already staked. I tried the Stewart River, but got nothing but frostbite. Then we came here. We were about to leave the Yukon. But we ran into a guy at the White Horse Hotel. He said he had a copper mine for sale. Rufus wasn't sure, but I told him we should try one more time. Criminy! The next day we sure felt stupid! We dug and blasted and hacked at the stone for weeks. All we got was blisters!"

He felt in his pocket. "Fruitcakes!" he said in annoyance. He looked at me. "I forgot that Rufus has it now. Anyway, then I found that nugget everyone is always talking about. The Lucky Eight! I found it right here! When we were digging this root cellar. Talk about lucky. I mean, gosh, there's not even supposed to be gold at Canyon City! Who knows how it got here. Some nasty ghost a million years ago. Anyway, what they say about it is true! I had Lucky Eight in my pocket the next time I was at the mine. Rufus was fixing to blast at the end of the tunnel. I told him to try ten feet to the left." He looked at me. "Well, guess what happened?"

"Rubies and diamonds?"

"I like your imagination, Papillon," he laughed. "No. But a streak of copper as thick as your leg!"

"You were rich!"

"That's exactly what I said to Rufus. We came back here to celebrate. I told him we could sell the mine and go back home. That's when he hit me with the frying pan."

"I thought he was your friend?"

"So did I! We'd been friends ever since our first day at the Cambridge Church School in Ontario! Other people never really liked him much, but he was always a pal to me. He liked being around when everyone was all chummy with me. I just didn't realize how much it made him hate me. Boy he said some mean things once I woke up down here."

"Why didn't he just kill you?" I asked.

"Well, he's a very religious fellow. You know how the Bible says 'Thou shalt not kill?' Well, he didn't want to murder me. That would be a sin. I told him he wasn't exactly being charitable by chaining me down here without food and water, but he just laughed and said it wouldn't be his fault if I 'expired.'"

"But why did he put the pancakes down here?"

"That was just cruelty. There's nothing in the Bible telling you not to put hot flapjacks, maple syrup from home and tall glass of milk just out of your friend's reach."

"Did he steal the Lucky Eight nugget?"

"Well, he's got it but he'd tell you he didn't steal it. Stealing's a sin too. So he took it from me but he's never sold it. It's still in a coffee tin with the rest of my gold hidden under his woodstove!"

"How do you know that?"

"Ghosts know these things." He sat silently for a minute. He was starting to look tired, if it's possible for ghosts to be tired.

"Can I help you at all?" I looked at the moldy pancakes. "Are you still hungry? I have some bread and cheese."

"No, thank you, Papillon. I can't eat now. I'm always hungry, but I can never eat. I just wish I could have one last meal then lie down and sleep in the soft brown earth, with some fireweed rustling in the wind above me." A glowing tear came out of his eye and fell to the floor. There was no water in it and it poofed into tiny glowing bits of dust before disappearing.

"Are you stuck here forever?"

"Did you read my poem upstairs?"

"Of course. It goes like this:

Greed, grudge, hatred and envy,
All these things can a friend be.
They are the curse that traps me here
Hidden in dark and frozen fear.
Oh the key, love in a stranger's sight
And knowing that Rufus Slight
Has felt Hell's hot bite."

He smiled a little bit. "It's not very good, is it."

"Oh no! It's very good," I lied.

"I heard your brothers joking that 'envy' and 'friend be' don't really rhyme. Honestly, it was the best I could do!"

"Is it Mr. Slight's envy and hatred that trap you here?" He nodded. "And how can you escape?"

"I never can, unless a stranger's love cancels out his hate."

"I'm a stranger."

"Well, yes. But Rufus also has to be brought to justice to make up for his betrayal of me. And I don't know how a little girl can do that."

I'd been thinking about that already.

"Yukon girls really are a little bit different," I said to myself a minute later as I ferried an old canoe across the river to the trail to Mr. Slight's cabin.

Aurore's journal

July 11th, 1902
Miles Canyon, Yukon Territory
9 a.m.

The Yukon morning cold woke me up early. I tried to squeeze left to cuddle with my sister Papillon but before I knew it I was touching the edge of the tent.

"Papillon's gone!" I cried.

My father and my brother Kip sat up immediately.

"What do you mean, gone?" asked Kip.

"You know what 'gone' means," I pointed out.

"How long has she been gone?" asked Papa.

"How should I know," replied Kip. "I've been asleep."

I stuck my hand deep into her sleeping robe. It was cold. "She's been gone for a couple of hours at least!"

Kip's brain started to move a bit faster. "She's gone back to Canyon City. She thinks the ghost can help us with the barn!"

"Ghost?" I said. "I can't believe anyone's taking Papillon's crazy story that seriously!"

Before I could say anything else, Kip sprang out from under his sleeping robe. He shoved his feet into his boots and sprinted for our horses. I saw immediately that Papillon's favourite horse Esprit was already gone.

Papa and I stumbled out of the tent just in time to see Kip toss a bridle onto Hootalinqua, our fastest horse. He untied the rope around her neck and, without even putting a saddle on, shouted "Let's go, Hoot!"

Hoot took off down the trail with Kip hanging around her neck. He banged both boots on the ground and bounced onto her back.

We watched him gallop away, wearing nothing but his pyjama bottoms and boots. He was crouched low on Hoot's back as if he was whispering "Faster!" in her ear.

"Hey!" cried Papa. "That was my horse!"

By now, the whole family was in an uproar. Our dog D'Artagnan went tearing out of camp following Kip and Hootalinqua. Papa and I quickly got dressed and tossed saddles onto our horses. Then I jumped onto Jasper and grabbed the reins. My little brother Yves ran for the food box and held out one of our food bags, which I grabbed as we went thundering by.

I've never ridden that fast in my life. But still, it seemed to take forever to get to Canyon City.

The whole way, I cursed myself for how rude I'd been to Papillon. I knew why she hadn't asked for help. It was because she thought I would make fun of her.

I flicked my reins onto Jasper's flank. "Faster! Faster!"

We rode fast. But Kip must have ridden even faster. When we got to Canyon City Hootalinqua was relaxing in the early morning mist by our cabin.

There was no one in the cabin, but Papa immediately spotted two canoes on the other side of the river. "Papillon's already across and Kip's gone after her!" We ran up and down the shore looking for another boat, but there weren't any.

Papa kicked a rock into the river in frustration.

Above: My sister Aurore riding Jasper as fast as she can to Canyon City in the middle of the night to come help me.

Journal #15

Editor's note: the journal starts again in Papillon's handwriting here

July 11th, 1902
Miles Canyon, Yukon Territory
Sitting beside Miles Canyon at 9 a.m.

It was still pretty dark when I got to Mr. Slight's cabin. I paused in the willows on the edge of the clearing. On my left, I could see the Yukon River tumbling past. And there was the dock where Kip must have dumped the logs in the water.

On my right were piles of mining equipment and a few sheds.

Straight ahead, I could see a big cabin with a new roof. I knew that had to be it.

Just beside the cabin there was a dog house. It probably belonged to Mr. Slight's evil dog Shadow. But how could I tell if the dog was really in there?

I crept closer. There was a stake in the ground in front of the dog house with a chain going through the door. I took another few steps. I had to hope that Shadow was chained.

And that the chain was short!

I sneaked up to the porch. Which planks would creak, I wondered? There were also a lot of noisy looking shovels and pickaxes lying around. Plus, what if Shadow's chain could actually reach the front door?

I took a step backwards and crept around the side of the cabin. The ground was mossy and silent. I quickly found what I was looking for, a window low enough for me to climb in.

I pulled out my pocket knife and slid the blade into the crack. I pressed my face to the glass until I could see the latch.

Above: Mr. Slight's cabin. You can see Shadow's doghouse plus the side window I used to sneak into the cabin.

"Click, click," it went each time I touched it with the knife, until suddenly it flipped over. It made what seemed like an enormous bang, but I'm sure you wouldn't even notice it unless you were sneaking around a murderer's cabin at night!

I slowly climbed in through the window. The cabin was exactly as Alastair had described it. I crawled into the bedroom. I could hear Mr. Slight breathing slowly and I could see the woodstove.

If Alastair was right then his coffee tin full of gold—including the Lucky Eight nugget—was hidden right underneath!

I crawled forward. There was a sheet of tin lying on the floor to protect it from cinders. I would have to move that, but first I had to get rid of the pile of firewood on top.

I reached past the stove to grab the first log. I gasped as I felt a sharp pain on my arm. The stove was still hot!

I rubbed the burn on my arm and looked around. Mr. Slight's breathing hadn't changed a bit. That was reassuring, but a little strange as I thought I had made enough noise to disturb him. I was expecting him to roll over at least.

I wondered for a moment why the stove was so hot. It should have burned down already, unless Mr. Slight had been staying up late.

I shrugged and went back to work.

There were a pair of leather gloves on top of the woodpile. They were singed and black from opening the stove when it was hot. I put those on, then picked up the wood piece by piece and very quietly moved it to the side.

Then it was time to move the tin. Now this was tricky, since there aren't many noisier things than sheets of tin. I looked around the room. There were a couple of Mr. Slight's shirts on a box, so I slid a sleeve under each leg of the stove.

Then, slowly, I started to slide the tin to the side. It hardly made a noise!

It got caught once on one of the legs, but if I pushed a little on the stove with my glove then I could move it a bit more.

Slowly, the sheet of tin slid sideways inch by inch.

I was about to run out of room, when suddenly I saw a hole in the wood. And in the hole, I could see a big can. On the side, I could see the words "Krinkhaus's Kingly Kamp Koffee."

"Alastair's gold!" I said to myself. I pulled it out carefully. "Perfect," I thought. "I didn't make a squeak the whole time." The can was heavy. I knew it was full of gold. To be safe, I decided to open it later.

I slowly moved the can over the tin sheet so I could pick it up.

"So you thought you could pull the wool over my eyes, did you?"

I gasped and turned around. Mr. Slight's eyes were wide open. He swung his feet out of bed. His face showed a combination of anger and fear.

"How did you know it was there?" he shouted. "Tell me!"

I decided to tell the truth.

"Alastair told me," I replied. His jaw dropped but somehow he didn't seem surprised. "Did you know he was still there?"

"Yes," said Mr. Slight bitterly. "Everyone kept telling me the cabin was haunted." He brooded for a minute. It seemed like forever. "Alastair was popular even after he died," he muttered finally.

I looked around to see if I could escape. But Mr. Slight was now between me and the window.

"Well," he said. "What to do with you? Does anyone know you're here?"

"No," I replied. I knew immediately that was a mistake. Mr. Slight smiled.

"Well," he said brusquely. "That solves that problem. Little girls drown in the Yukon River all the time. Tragic, of course, but it happens." He grimaced. "I can't possibly let you go back and tell everyone where Alastair is." He looked down at the coffee can. "Or where the Lucky Eight nugget is, for that matter." He sat down on his bed. "Put another log on the fire while I get dressed," he snapped. "It's frigid up here even in the summer!"

Journal #16

July 11th, 1902
Miles Canyon, Yukon Territory
Sitting beside Miles Canyon at 9:30 a.m.

I kneeled in front of the woodstove. I was really in trouble now. How could I get away?

I heard a voice outside. "Ah," said Mr. Slight. "That'll be Red McGraw. He'll be happy to take you for a quick little canoe ride."

I stared at him in horror.

"Come on," he snapped. "I told you to put more wood on the fire." I was still too frozen to move. "Now that's why I hate children! Too stupid for even the simplest tasks." He stood up and moved towards me.

Suddenly, I knew what to do. I opened the woodstove door. Then, instead of putting in a log, I jammed my glove deep into the coals. In one quick move, I hurled a giant handful right into Mr. Slight's face.

"Aaahhhhh!" he screamed. I grabbed the can and ran for the front door. I looked back over my shoulder to see him jump up and come after me. But he took just one step before I saw his bare foot land on a red hot coal.

There was a horrible sizzling noise and he fell to the floor screaming.

I yanked open the door and ran onto the porch.

But there was Red McGraw! And Shadow was right beside him!

"What's this?" said Red McGraw, with a nasty grin. "Stealing my
boss's, err, coffee?" He was puzzled, but only for a second.

I was cornered. I shrank back, clutching the coffee tin.

Shadow growled and moved towards me.

Suddenly I saw a flash of brown and white and heard a vicious
snarl.

It was D'Artagnan! He leaped onto Shadow like a wolf, knocking
him right into the cabin! Instantly the two dogs were rolling like a ball
of howling devils, snapping at each other and growling in fury.

Then Red McGraw and I saw something even more surprising.
Right on D'Artagnan's heels came Kip! He wasn't wearing anything
but his pyjamas!

"Let my sister go!" he said.

Red laughed. "Run!" shouted Kip, so I took off for the river. I saw
Kip and Red McGraw circle each other in front of the cabin. They
were both crouched with their hands in front of them. They stared
into each other's eyes savagely as they looked for a chance to
pounce. It was just like when Kip fought Zeke Henderson at school,
but Red McGraw was four times bigger than Zeke!

Suddenly Red lunged with his arms. But Kip was faster. He
dropped to the ground and rolled out of the way, knocking over a
bucket of axe handles. "Crackerjack!" he exclaimed as he
grabbed one and leaped to his feet.

Red McGraw grabbed one too. "So you're a sword fighter are
you, little fella?" he said with a sneer.

Red McGraw took a mighty swing at Kip's body, but Kip just
jumped back. Then Red lunged forward, but Kip parried. This made
Red really angry and he launched a furious attack, swinging his axe
handle left and right.

"Watch out!" I shouted as a blow just missed Kip's face.

"Don't wait for me!" shouted Kip. "Run!"

Then Red McGraw attacked again. Kip was standing just like Sam Steele taught him. He dodged or parried every attack.

I knew he was just waiting for his chance.

Suddenly Red McGraw made a mighty swing, just like a lumberjack. Splinters flew off Kip's axe handle as he parried the blow. But now the big man was off balance. In the blink of an eye, Kip lunged forward as far as he could reach.

"Ooof!" gasped Red McGraw as Kip's axe handle sank into his stomach. He doubled over in pain. Before he could recover, Kip slipped right and swung hard and low like a baseball batter.

I saw the axe handle connect with Red McGraw's left knee.

There was a horrible crunching noise. He yelped and hit the ground with the thud of a giant sausage.

Kip turned. "Run! Run!" He took a step towards me, but then saw Mr. Slight come out of the cabin. Instead, he took off in the opposite direction with D'Artagnan at his heels. Shadow was right after them, with Red McGraw hobbling behind.

"Not them!" shouted Mr. Slight. "The girl. Get that stupid girl!"

He started running towards me. I could see he had his gun. I ran down to the dock and jumped in his canoe. I brought an axe down on the rope and felt the river grab the canoe.

I crawled to the middle and grabbed a paddle. I quickly steered towards the middle of the river, where the current was stronger.

I could see Mr. Slight on the dock, waving his gun at me. Then I saw him run back to shore and grab another canoe.

"Why didn't I cut the rope on that one too?" I shouted to myself as I paddled.

I looked back to see Mr. Slight gaining on me. I paddled harder, but it was very difficult to keep the canoe straight with just one paddler.

Fortunately, Mr. Slight wasn't a very good paddler either. His canoe kept weaving left and right. He was so mad that he was paddling as hard as he could. That was actually good for me, since when he tried too hard his strokes would send his canoe spinning off course.

I kept paddling.

I had to admit, though, that he was gaining. "You won't get away this time!" he was shouting. Once he put down his paddle and pulled out his gun. I kept paddling. The noise was unbelievably loud. Shooting a gun is nowhere near as loud as having one shot at you!

I heard the bullet whiz by. I heard two more shots, then saw him back at his paddle. Unfortunately, he was getting the hang of it. His canoe was pointed straight at me.

I kept paddling.

I came around the corner and could see Canyon City in the distance.

Someone was on the shore. It was Aurore! She spotted me and seemed to freeze.

Editor's note: the next section of the journal was glued in place and appears to be in Aurore's handwriting not Papillon's

I looked up river and froze in surprise! It was Papillon in a canoe. A second later, Mr. Slight came around the corner behind her.

He was waving a gun!

A hundred thoughts went through my mind. Run away! Why was Papillon always getting us in trouble? Why did she always have to make up those crazy ghost stories?

Then another thought hit me.

Maybe I should trust my sister.

Maybe the ghost really did exist!

I turned on my heels and ran for the cabin. "Hey ghost!" I shouted. "Papillon's in trouble!"

Nothing happened.

"Mr. Ghost! Papillon's in trouble! And it's because of you!"

Still nothing happened. I banged my foot on the floor in frustration. Then I noticed that one of the planks I had stomped had moved. There was a gap in the floor!

I banged my foot again. "Are you down there Mr. Ghost?"

Suddenly, a greenish mist came out of the floor. "Is that you, Papillon?" said a strange voice.

I stood up in amazement as the mist turned into a ghost right in front of me. "I ... I ... I can't believe it!" I stammered. Then I recovered myself. "Papillon's in trouble! Mr. Slight's chasing her on the river!"

The ghost moved to the window in a flash. "Rufus!" he cried. It was like he was in pain. He looked back at me. "Papillon!" he said.

"Well, go help her!" I said.

"I'm not supposed to leave the cabin at this time of day. It's against the rules." He looked down at his ghostly feet.

I reached out the grab his arm, but my hand just went through him. "Well, you've got to go anyway!" I cried. "She needs you!"

He seemed to pull himself together. "You're right. It's time I did something useful." He turned and walked right through the wall.

I took a step after him before remembering that I had to use the door. Then I ran after him and saw him floating swiftly across the rocks turning into mist as he went.

By the time I got to the edge of the water I couldn't see him anywhere!

"Help her!" I shrieked, running back and forth between the water and the cabin. But the ghost was gone!

Editor's note: the journal continues here in Papillon's handwriting

I was close to Canyon City now. I could see Papa and Aurore on the shore shouting. They were telling me to land.

But I could also hear Mr. Slight screaming behind me. I glanced back to see him waving his gun again, telling me to stop.

If I landed the canoe, he might shoot Papa! But if I stayed on the river, it would take me right through the rapids of Miles Canyon and the Devil's Punchbowl!

I could already hear their roar.

I looked at Aurore and Papa, then at Mr. Slight, then at the spray and waves of Miles Canyon up ahead.

I had never canoed something like that before.

Then I heard a voice! It sounded like Alastair's. "You can do it, Papillon!"

"No, I can't," I thought.

I could see Papa and Aurore on the shore. I was almost there.

Then I heard a gunshot and a bullet whiz by.

I looked again at Papa and Aurore. "I can do it," I said. "I have to."

I stuck my paddle into the Yukon River and turned the canoe. Its nose headed straight for the opening of Miles Canyon.

"No!" shouted Papa.

The river went faster and faster. I could feel the ripples grab at the canoe as the water sped up. The roaring of the rapids got louder.

So did the shouting of Mr. Slight. He was right behind me!

I felt my canoe shudder as the water began to tumble into Miles Canyon. There was no going back now!

Waves tossed my canoe back and forth. The spray was every-where and the noise was unbelievably loud.

I desperately paddled left then right to keep my canoe pointed down the middle.

A whirlpool suddenly grabbed my canoe and turned it sharply left. I was headed right for the Canyon wall and a giant, jagged rock.

"Ha ha!" I heard Mr. Slight shout. His canoe was just behind mine.

The rock was right in front of me. A wave welled up, lifting my canoe. It was about to smash me into the canyon wall!

Suddenly, I felt something else in the canoe. The nose turned suddenly down the river. I looked behind me. There was Alastair at the back, with his glowing paddle deep in the water. "Paddle!" he shouted.

I pushed off the rock and paddled like I'd never paddled before.

"Pry!" he shouted. I jabbed my paddle into the water, just like Papa taught me. Then Alastair shouted "Draw!" My paddle flew back and forth.

We shot out of Miles Canyon into the Devil's Punchbowl, with our canoe dodging the giant whirlpool like Alastair was steering a toy boat in the bathtub.

Suddenly I felt a rope land on me. "Grab it!" shouted Aurore on the shore just beside me. I tossed her the coffee tin and jumped onto the rocks. The canoe was empty.

"Where's Alastair?" I cried as another wave grabbed my empty canoe and tossed it back into the current.

"Look!" shouted Aurore, barely loud enough to be heard over the roaring water.

I looked back up the river into Miles Canyon. I could see Mr. Slight's canoe smash into the canyon wall again and again. It was half full of water and his paddle was broken in his hands. Then his canoe bounced free.

It swept down into the giant whirlpool. He grabbed the broken blade of his paddle and smashed it into the water.

All of a sudden, his canoe seemed to stop. "It's going backwards!" cried Aurore. And it was!

We watched in horror as it moved slowly backwards as if drawn by a giant invisible hand. Then, in a giant splash, its front end tilted up and it disappeared into the whirlpool with Mr. Slight screaming "No Alastair!" as it went.

Journal #17

July 21st, 1902
Canyon City, Yukon Territory
Beside the fireweed patch at Canyon City just after dawn

I pulled out my journal and opened it to Alastair's poem. I straightened my best dress and tried to knock a bit of Yukon River clay off my boots.

You want to look your best at a funeral.

My family was standing around a grave that Kip and Papa had dug. A plain wooden coffin was lying beside the hole. It still smelled of spruce, since Papa and I had just finished it the day before in our barn.

"I'm glad we're doing this," I had said to Papa. "After all, there was more than enough gold in Alastair's coffee tin to pay back the bank and keep the barn."

Papa had smiled. "I was thinking more about him helping your canoe through Miles Canyon."

We all stood beside the grave thinking quietly. I reached into my pocket and felt for the Lucky Eight nugget.

The fireweed rustled in the breeze and, in the distance, I could see a faint curl of woodsmoke rise out of our cabin's chimney.

I began to read.

Greed, grudge, hatred and envy,
All these things can a friend be.
They are the curse that traps me here
Hidden in dark and frozen fear.
Oh the key, love in a stranger's sight
And knowing that Rufus Slight
Has felt Hell's hot bite.

"I hope that brings you peace, Alastair," I said. "We picked a spot in the fireweed just like you wanted." There was a tear in my eye. We were all crying, even Papa.

I walked over to the coffin and put the Lucky Eight nugget and a canoe paddle on top. We didn't say anything as we grabbed the ropes and lowered Alastair into the ground.

After he was buried, we sat quietly on the edge of Miles Canyon for a long time. The light was just starting to streak over Grey Mountain and the mist was floating over the river, just like my first morning in Canyon City.

"Kip," I said finally. "Do you think we did it right? Will that poem really release him from haunting that little root cellar?"

"I imagine so. That's what he told you," said Kip with a nod. "It felt right, anyway."

"I just hope he's happy now, wherever his spirit is."

We sat for a bit longer. Another streak of sunlight came over Grey Mountain. Suddenly we heard a strange noise. "Was that someone saying 'yippee?'" asked Yves.

"Look!" I cried. We watched in amazement as the mist on the river formed into a shape. It was a man in a canoe. And as he went by he waved his hat to us.

"I guess it didn't work," I said.

"Something did," Kip replied as the canoe disappeared down the river. "Alastair was smiling as he tipped his hat to you."

About This Book

This book is historical fiction, with an invented storyline and characters set among true historical events and characters.

Canyon City was indeed a gold rush town just above Miles Canyon on the Yukon River that was abandoned by 1902. You can visit it today, a short hike from Miles Canyon. It is sometimes confused with Canyon City, Alaska, on the Chilkoot Trail. Will Drury and Sam Steele are true historical figures. All of the photos are real, drawn from the MacBride Museum or the author's family collection. The historical events and characters are portrayed as accurately as possible, based on what we know today.

But Papillon Dutoit and her family are fictional, as are Rufus Slight and Alastair Riveridge. Red McGraw and Hard Luck Henry are characters drawn from Robert Service's poems, as is the story of how Hard Luck Henry met the twins and their mother.

The reader can visit Canyon City and decide whether the Yukon River ghost really exists or not.

The Dutoit family is inspired by the author's pioneering ancestors, the Cyrs. Papa is based on Antoine Cyr, an Acadian who arrived in the Yukon in 1898 with his brother Michel. Tony and Mike, as they were soon known in anglophone Whitehorse, were well suited to life in the Yukon thanks to their experience in the rivers and lumberyards of New Brunswick. After guiding many goldseekers (including Jack London, as mentioned in *Yukon River Ghost*) through Miles Canyon and the White Horse rapids, they stayed in Whitehorse running a wood business and constructing log buildings such as the Old Log Church Rectory and Cyr House.

Aurore's story parallels that of the author's grandmother, Aline (Cyr) Taylor. She was a young girl in Montreal when her father died. She, her mother Marie-Ange and little brother Wilbrod moved to the Yukon to join their uncle at Kirkman Creek. The uncle had sent many letters describing Kirkman Creek as a thriving community of which he was a leading (and rich) member. He may even have claimed to have been its mayor. Aurore took the train with her mother and brother from Montreal to Vancouver, a ship to Skagway, the train to Whitehorse and went by river to Kirkman Creek. The log cabin, dirt floor and empty larder they found in Kirkman Creek were a shock after living in Montreal. They decided to leave the Yukon.

After struggling with English-speaking ticket agents as portrayed in *Aurore of the Yukon*, the ticket agent sent for Tony Cyr to help translate. While Tony helped with the translation, he also convinced Marie-Ange to marry him.

Aline stayed in the Yukon for the rest of her life, helping raise five half-brothers and sisters and eventually her own family with Bill Taylor of the pioneer merchants Taylor & Drury.

Cyrs, Taylors and Drurys can be found across the North, from Skagway to Tagish to Whitehorse. Pascale and Aline Halliday, the fifth generation since the gold rush pioneers, illustrated this book.

Acknowledgments

The author is grateful to acknowledge the assistance of so many who gave their help so freely.

Aline and Bill Taylor, my grandparents, for filling my life with Yukon stories

Kieran, Aline, Pascale and Ewan, my children, for inspiring the story and Stacy for putting up with a prolonged bout of ghost mania

Alice and Paul Cyr for a fine dinner at Tagish as the final chapter was written

Johanne Papillon and Stéphane Aucoin for French advice

Geoff Smith for historical and editing advice

Ken Quong and Aldea Wood on the cover photo

Patricia Cunning, Alexis Jensen and Tracey Anderson at the MacBride Museum for historical, costume and moral support

Juliann Fraser for editorial advice

Emily Ross, Hero and Storm Scott, Sean and Nicola Purcell, Noah Clark, Spencer Quong, Pia Blake, Leif Blake, Galena Roots, Ingrid Janzen for early reviews and encouragement

Suggestions and assistance from Kyle Janzen, Mary-Anne Roots, Meera Sarin and others

About the Author

Keith Halliday is passionate about Yukon history. He was born in the Yukon and raised on stories of the pioneer days. He is a descendent of the Taylors and Drurys, gold rush era merchants and fur traders. His great-grandmother was Marie-Ange Cyr, who moved in 1917 from Montreal to the Yukon frontier with her children Aline and Wilbrod after her husband died. The story of Marie-Ange, Aline and Wilbrod was the inspiration for the *Aurore of the Yukon* series.

After detours in the diplomatic service in Brussels, study in London and management consulting in Toronto, Keith and his wife Stacy live with their four children in the Yukon, where they intend to stay.

About the Illustrators

Pascale and Aline Halliday are fifth generation Yukoners. They live with their parents in Whitehorse, not far from the locations in this book. In the winter, they often ski along the old tramway trail to Canyon City, Miles Canyon and the Devil's Punchbowl.

They are already working on the pictures for the next adventures of Aurore, Kip, Papillon and Yves.

About the MacBride Museum

MacBride Museum is the Yukon's first museum. It is a fun, interactive and educational institution that illustrates the overall history of the Yukon. Located on Whitehorse's scenic waterfront at the corner of 1st Avenue and Wood Street, MacBride is open year round. Its galleries explore Yukon Facts and Myths, The Natural World of animals and minerals, a hands-on Discovery Zone for kids, Yukon First Nations plus transportation and mining history. Recently opened, the MacBride's new galleries outline the Yukon's modern history from early exploration in the 1800's until Whitehorse became the capital of the Yukon in 1953.

Go to *www.macbridemuseum.com* to find out more about MacBride's programs, events, online collection and activities, including MacBride Museum summer camps based on the books in the Yukon Kids Series: *Aurore of the Yukon, Yukon Secret Agents* and *Yukon River Ghost.*

Also available
in the
MacBride Museum
Yukon Kids Series

Aurore of the Yukon: A Girl's Adventure in the Klondike Gold Rush

"She's just a girl!" shouted Windy Bill.

When Aurore hears these words, she knows notorious Alaskan bandit Soapy Smith is about to find out everything. How will she get her mother's money back now? How will she expose Soapy and his gang? Even worse, how will she escape?

Aurore, her mother and little brother have set off for Uncle Thibault's lodge in the Yukon after the death of Aurore's father, little knowing they are headed for the Klondike gold rush and the adventure of a lifetime.

Aurore must dig deeper, think harder and be braver than she ever thought possible to show Soapy and his gang what a girl—and her new Tlingit friend Louise and a Yukon river boy named Kip—can do.

"Well, she outsmarted you!" replied Soapy Smith, opening the door to Aurore's hiding place ...

Set in the historic Klondike gold rush of 1898, and inspired a real girl's adventure, *Aurore of the Yukon* is an exciting adventure written to both entertain and educate young readers.

~   ~   ~

Yukon Secret Agents: A Boy's Adventure during the Alaska Border Dispute

Aurore and Kip are back, this time as secret agents!

The Klondike gold rush is over and Yukon kids are adjusting to normal life. But life is never normal in the Yukon.

It's the summer of 1903. School is almost out ... and Canada, Britain and the United States are on the brink of war over the Alaskan border. This doesn't mean much to Kip and Aurore, until a deadly explosion at the Star Mine throws them into a swirling adventure involving coded telegrams, burgled hotel rooms and President Teddy Roosevelt ... and a mysterious German naval captain named Oskar von Neidling.

Can Kip and Aurore find out the truth—and stop the villains—before it's too late?

978-0-595-49364-7
0-595-49364-5

LaVergne, TN USA
07 April 2010
178381LV00001B/17/P